EVERY HEART
A DOORWAY

ALSO BY SEANAN McGUIRE

EVERY HEART
A DOORWAY

SEANAN
McGUIRE

A TOM DOHERTY ASSOCIATES BOOK

NEW YORK

EVERY HEART A DOORWAY

Copyright © 2016 by Seanan McGuire

A Tor.com Book
Published by Tom Doherty Associates, LLC
175 Fifth Avenue
New York, NY 10010

www.tor-forge.com

Tor® is a registered trademark of Tom Doherty Associates, LLC.

The Library of Congress Cataloging-in-Publication Data
is available upon request.

ISBN 978-0-7653-8550-5 (hardcover)
ISBN 978-0-7653-8387-7 (e-book)

Our books may be purchased in bulk for promotional, educational, or business use. Please contact your local bookseller or the Macmillan Corporate and Premium Sales Department at (800) 221-7945, extension 5442, or by e-mail at MacmillanSpecialMarkets@macmillan.com.

First Edition: April 2016

Printed in the United States of America

0 9 8 7

FOR THE WICKED

PART I

THE GOLDEN AFTERNOONS

THERE WAS A LITTLE GIRL

THE GIRLS WERE NEVER present for the entrance interviews. Only their parents, their guardians, their confused siblings, who wanted so much to help them but didn't know how. It would have been too hard on the prospective students to sit there and listen as the people they loved most in all the world—all this world, at least—dismissed their memories as delusions, their experiences as fantasy, their lives as some intractable illness.

What's more, it would have damaged their ability to trust the school if their first experience of Eleanor had been seeing her dressed in respectable grays and lilacs, with her hair styled just so, like the kind of stolid elderly aunt who only really existed in children's stories. The real Eleanor was nothing like that. Hearing the things she said would have only made it worse, as she sat there and explained, so earnestly, so sincerely, that her school would help to cure the things that had gone wrong in the minds of all those little lost lambs. She could take the broken children and make them whole again.

She was lying, of course, but there was no way for her potential students to know that. So she demanded that she meet with their legal guardians in private, and she sold her bill of goods with the focus and skill of a born con artist. If those guardians had ever come together to compare notes, they would have found that her script was well-practiced and honed like the weapon that it was.

"This is a rare but not unique disorder that manifests in young girls just stepping across the border into woman-hood," she would say, making careful eye contact with the desperate, overwhelmed guardians of her latest wandering girl. On the rare occasion when she had to speak to the parents of a boy, she would vary her speech, but only as much as the situation demanded. She had been working on this routine for a long time, and she knew how to play upon the fears and desires of adults. They wanted what was best for their charges, as did she. It was simply that they had very different ideas of what "best" meant.

To the parents, she said, "This is a delusion, and some time away may help to cure it."

To the aunts and uncles, she said, "This is not your fault, and I can be the solution."

To the grandparents, she said, "Let me help. Please, let me help you."

Not every family agreed on boarding school as the best

solution. About one out of every three potential students slipped through her fingers, and she mourned for them, those whose lives would be so much harder than they needed to be, when they could have been saved. But she rejoiced for those who were given to her care. At least while they were with her, they would be with someone who understood. Even if they would never have the opportunity to go back home, they would have someone who understood, and the company of their peers, which was a treasure beyond reckoning.

Eleanor West spent her days giving them what she had never had, and hoped that someday, it would be enough to pay her passage back to the place where she belonged.

1 COMING HOME, LEAVING HOME

THE HABIT OF NARRATION, of crafting something miraculous out of the commonplace, was hard to break. Narration came naturally after a time spent in the company of talking scarecrows or disappearing cats; it was, in its own way, a method of keeping oneself grounded, connected to the thin thread of continuity that ran through all lives, no matter how strange they might become. Narrate the impossible things, turn them into a story, and they could be controlled. So:

The manor sat in the center of what would have been considered a field, had it not been used to frame a private home. The grass was perfectly green, the trees clustered around the structure perfectly pruned, and the garden grew in a profusion of colors that normally existed together only in a rainbow, or in a child's toy box. The thin black ribbon of the driveway curved from the distant gate to form a loop in front of the manor itself, feeding elegantly into a slightly wider waiting area at the base of the porch. A single car pulled up, tawdry yellow and seeming somehow shabby against the carefully curated scene. The rear passenger door slammed, and the car pulled away again, leaving a teenage girl behind.

She was tall and willowy and couldn't have been more than seventeen; there was still something of the unformed around her eyes and mouth, leaving her a work in progress, meant to be finished by time. She wore black—black jeans, black ankle boots with tiny black buttons marching like soldiers from toe to calf—and she wore white—a loose tank top, the faux pearl bands around her wrists—and she had a ribbon the color of pomegranate seeds tied around the base of her ponytail. Her hair was bone-white streaked with runnels of black, like oil spilled on a marble floor, and her eyes were pale as ice. She squinted in the daylight. From the look of her, it had been quite some time since she had seen the sun. Her small wheeled suitcase was bright pink, covered with cartoon daisies. She had not, in all likelihood, purchased it herself.

Raising her hand to shield her eyes, the girl looked toward the manor, pausing when she saw the sign that hung from the porch eaves. ELEANOR WEST'S HOME FOR WAYWARD CHILDREN it read, in large letters. Below, in smaller letters, it continued NO SOLICITATION, NO VISITORS, NO QUESTS.

The girl blinked. The girl lowered her hand. And slowly, the girl made her way toward the steps.

On the third floor of the manor, Eleanor West let go of the curtain and turned toward the door while the fabric was still fluttering back into its original position. She appeared to be a well-preserved woman in her late sixties, although her true age was closer to a hundred: travel through the lands she had once frequented had a tendency to scramble the internal clock, making it difficult for time to get a proper grip upon the body. Some days she was grateful for her longevity, which had allowed her to help so many more children than she would ever have lived to see if she hadn't opened the doors she had, if she had never chosen to stray from her proper path. Other days, she wondered whether this world would ever discover that she existed—that she was little Ely West the Wayward Girl, somehow alive after all these years— and what would happen to her when that happened.

Still, for the time being, her back was strong and her eyes were as clear as they had been on the day when, as a girl of seven, she had seen the opening between the roots of a tree on her father's estate. If her hair was white now, and her skin was soft with wrinkles and memories, well, that was no matter at all. There was still something unfinished around her eyes; she wasn't done yet. She was a story, not an epilogue. And if she chose to narrate her own life one word at a time as she descended the stairs to meet her newest arrival, that wasn't hurting anyone. Narration was a hard habit to break, after all.

Sometimes it was all a body had.

NANCY STOOD FROZEN in the center of the foyer, her hand locked on the handle of her suitcase as she looked around, trying to find her bearings. She wasn't sure what she'd been expecting from the "special school" her parents were sending her to, but it certainly hadn't been this . . . this elegant country home. The walls were papered in an old-fashioned floral print of roses and twining clematis vines, and the furnishings—such as they were in this intentionally under-furnished entryway—were all antiques, good, well-polished wood with brass fittings that matched the curving sweep of the banister. The floor was cherrywood, and when she glanced upward, trying to move her eyes without lifting her chin, she found herself looking at an elaborate chandelier shaped like a blooming flower.

"That was made by one of our alumni, actually," said a voice. Nancy wrenched her gaze from the chandelier and turned it toward the stairs.

The woman who was descending was thin, as elderly women sometimes were, but her back was straight, and the hand resting on the banister seemed to be using it only as a guide, not as any form of support. Her hair was as white as Nancy's own, without the streaks of defiant black, and styled in a puffbull of a perm, like a dandelion that had gone to seed. She would have looked perfectly respectable, if not for her electric orange trousers, paired with a hand-knit sweater knit of rainbow wool and a necklace of semiprecious stones in a dozen colors, all of them clashing. Nancy felt her eyes widen despite her best efforts, and hated herself for it. She was losing hold of her stillness one day at a time.

Soon, she would be as jittery and unstable as any of the living, and then she would never find her way back home.

"It's virtually all glass, of course, except for the bits that aren't," continued the woman, seemingly untroubled by Nancy's blatant staring. "I'm not at all sure how you make that sort of thing. Probably by melting sand, I assume. I contributed those large teardrop-shaped prisms at the center, however. All twelve of them were of my making. I'm rather proud of that." The woman paused, apparently expecting Nancy to say something.

Nancy swallowed. Her throat was so *dry* these days, and nothing seemed to chase the dust away. "If you don't know how to make glass, how did you make the prisms?" she asked.

The woman smiled. "Out of my tears, of course. Always assume the simplest answer is the true one, here, because most of the time, it will be. I'm Eleanor West. Welcome to my home. You must be Nancy."

"Yes," Nancy said slowly. "How did you . . . ?"

"Well, you're the only student we were expecting to receive today. There aren't as many of you as there once were. Either the doors are getting rarer, or you're all getting better about not coming back. Now, be quiet a moment, and let me look at you." Eleanor descended the last three steps and stopped in front of Nancy, studying her intently for a moment before she walked a slow circle around her. "Hmm. Tall, thin, and very pale. You must have been someplace with no sun—but no vampires either, I think, given the skin on your neck. Jack and Jill will be awfully pleased to meet you. They get tired of all the sunlight and sweetness people bring through here."

"Vampires?" said Nancy blankly. "Those aren't real."

"None of this is *real,* my dear. Not this house, not this conversation, not those shoes you're wearing—which are several years out of style if you're trying to reacclimatize yourself to the ways of your peers, and are not proper mourning shoes if you're trying to hold fast to your recent past—and not either one of us. 'Real' is a four-letter word, and I'll thank you to use it as little as possible while you live under my roof." Eleanor stopped in front of Nancy again. "It's the hair that betrays you. Were you in an Underworld or a Netherworld? You can't have been in an Afterlife. No one comes back from those."

Nancy gaped at her, mouth moving silently as she tried to find her voice. The old woman said those things—those cruelly impossible things—so casually, like she was asking after nothing more important than Nancy's vaccination records.

Eleanor's expression transformed, turning soft and apologetic. "Oh, I see I've upset you. I'm afraid I have a tendency to do that. I went to a Nonsense world, you see, six times before I turned sixteen, and while I eventually had to stop crossing over, I never quite learned to rein my tongue back in. You must be tired from your journey, and curious about what's to happen here. Is that so? I can show you to your room as soon as I know where you fall on the compass. I'm afraid that really does matter for things like housing; you can't put a Nonsense traveler in with someone who went walking through Logic, not unless you feel like explaining a remarkable amount of violence to the local police. They *do* check up on us here, even if we can usually get them to look the other way. It's all part of our remaining accredited as a school, although I suppose we're more of a sanitarium, of sorts. I do like that word, don't you? 'Sanitarium.' It sounds so official, while meaning absolutely nothing at all."

"I don't understand anything you're saying right now," said Nancy. She was ashamed to hear her voice come out in a tinny squeak, even as she was proud of herself for finding it at all.

Eleanor's face softened further. "You don't have to pretend anymore, Nancy. I know what you've been going through—where you've been. I went through something a long time ago, when I came back from my own voyages. This isn't a place for lies or pretending everything is all right. We know everything is not all right. If it were, you wouldn't be here. Now. Where did you go?"

"I don't . . ."

"Forget about words like 'Nonsense' and 'Logic.' We can work out those details later. Just answer. Where did you *go?*"

"I went to the Halls of the Dead." Saying the words aloud was an almost painful relief. Nancy froze again, staring into space as if she could see her voice hanging there, shining garnet-dark and perfect in the air. Then she swallowed, still not chasing away the dryness, and said, "It was . . . I was looking for a bucket in the cellar of our house, and I found this door I'd never seen before. When I went through, I was in a grove of pomegranate trees. I thought I'd fallen and hit my head. I kept going because . . . because . . ."

Because the air had smelled so sweet, and the sky had been black velvet, spangled with points of diamond light that didn't flicker at all, only burned constant and cold. Because the grass had been wet with dew, and the trees had been heavy with fruit. Because she had wanted to know what was at the end of the long path between the trees, and because she hadn't wanted to turn back before she understood everything. Because for the first time in forever, she'd felt like she was going home, and that feeling had been enough to move her feet, slowly at first, and then faster, and faster, until she had been running through the clean night air, and nothing else had mattered, or would ever matter again—

"How long were you gone?"

The question was meaningless. Nancy shook her head. "Forever. Years . . . I was there for years. I didn't want to come back. Ever."

"I know, dear." Eleanor's hand was gentle on Nancy's elbow, guiding her toward the door behind the stairs. The old woman's perfume smelled of dandelions and gingersnaps, a combination as nonsensical as everything else about her. "Come with me. I have the perfect room for you."

ELEANOR'S "PERFECT ROOM" was on the first floor, in the shadow of a great old elm that blocked almost all the light that would otherwise have come in through the single window. It was eternal twilight in that room, and Nancy felt the weight drop from her shoulders as she stepped inside and looked around. One half of the room—the half with the window—was a jumble of clothing, books, and knick-knacks. A fiddle was tossed carelessly on the bed, and the associated bow was balanced on the edge of the book-shelf, ready to fall at the slightest provocation. The air smelled of mint and mud.

The other half of the room was as neutral as a hotel. There was a bed, a small dresser, a bookshelf, and a desk, all in pale, unvarnished wood. The walls were blank. Nancy looked to Eleanor long enough to receive the nod of approval before walking over and placing her suitcase primly in the middle of what would be her bed.

"Thank you," she said. "I'm sure this will be fine."

"I admit, I'm not as confident," said Eleanor, frowning at Nancy's suitcase. It had been placed so *precisely*. . . . "Anyplace called 'the Halls of the Dead' is going to have been an Underworld, and most of those fall more under the banner of Nonsense than Logic. It seems like yours may have been more regimented. Well, no matter. We can always move you if you and Sumi prove ill-suited. Who knows? You might provide her with some of the grounding she currently lacks. And if you can't do that, well, hopefully you won't actually kill one another."

"Sumi?"

"Your roommate." Eleanor picked her way through the mess on the floor until she reached the window. Pushing it open, she leaned out and scanned the branches of the elm tree until she found what she was looking for. "One and two and three, I see you, Sumi. Come inside and meet your roommate."

"Roommate?" The voice was female, young, and annoyed.

"I warned you," said Eleanor as she pulled her head back inside and returned to the center of the room. She moved with remarkable assurance, especially given how cluttered the floor was; Nancy kept expecting her to fall, and somehow, she didn't. "I told you a new student was arriving this week, and that if it was a girl from a compatible background, she would be taking the spare bed. Do you remember any of this?"

"I thought you were just talking to hear yourself talk. You *do* that. Everyone *does* that." A head appeared in the window, upside down, its owner apparently hanging from the elm tree. She looked to be about Nancy's age, of Japanese descent, with long black hair tied into two childish pigtails, one above each ear. She looked at Nancy with unconcealed suspicion before asking, "Are you a servant of the Queen of Cakes, here to punish me for my transgressions against the Countess of Candy Floss? Because I don't feel like going to war right now."

"No," said Nancy blankly. "I'm Nancy."

"That's a boring name. How can you be here with such a boring name?" Sumi flipped around and dropped out of the tree, vanishing for a moment before she popped back up, leaned on the windowsill, and asked, "Eleanor-Ely, are you *sure*? I mean, sure-sure? She doesn't look like she's supposed to be here at *all*. Maybe when you looked at her records, you saw what wasn't there again and really she's supposed to be in a school for juvenile victims of bad dye jobs."

"I don't dye my hair!" Nancy's protest was heated. Sumi stopped talking and blinked at her. Eleanor turned to look at her. Nancy's cheeks grew hot as the blood rose in her face, but she stood her ground, somehow keeping herself from reaching up to stroke her hair as she said, "It used to be all black, like my mother's. When I danced with the Lord of the Dead for the first time, he said it was beautiful, and he ran his fingers through it. All the hair turned white around them, out of jealousy. That's why I only have five black streaks left. Those are the parts he touched."

Looking at her with a critical eye, Eleanor could see how those five streaks formed the phantom outline of a hand, a place where the pale young woman in front of her had been touched once and never more. "I see," she said.

"I don't *dye* it," said Nancy, still heated. "I would never *dye* it. That would be disrespectful."

Sumi was still blinking, eyes wide and round. Then she grinned. "Oh, I *like* you," she said. "You're the craziest card in the deck, aren't you?"

"We don't use that word here," snapped Eleanor.

"But it's true," said Sumi. "She thinks she's going back. Don't you, *Nancy*? You think you're going to open the right-wrong door and see your stairway to Heaven on the other side, and then it's one step, two step, how d'you do step, and you're right back in your story. Crazy girl. *Stupid* girl. You can't go back. Once they throw you out, you can't go back."

Nancy felt as if her heart were trying to scramble up her throat and choke her. She swallowed it back down, and said, in a whisper, "You're wrong."

Sumi's eyes were bright. "Am I?"

Eleanor clapped her hands, pulling their attention back to her. "Nancy, why don't you unpack and get settled? Dinner is at six thirty, and group therapy will follow at eight. Sumi, please don't inspire her to murder you before she's been here for a full day."

"We all have our own ways of trying to go home," said Sumi, and disappeared from the window's frame, heading off to whatever she'd been doing before Eleanor disturbed her. Eleanor shot Nancy a quick, apologetic look, and then she too was gone, shutting the door behind herself. Nancy was, quite abruptly, alone.

She stayed where she was for a count of ten, enjoying the stillness. When she had been in the Halls of the Dead, she had sometimes been expected to hold her position for days at a time, blending in with the rest of the living statuary. Serving girls who were less skilled at stillness had come through with sponges soaked in pomegranate juice and sugar, pressing them to the lips of the unmoving. Nancy had learned to let the juice trickle down her throat without swallowing, taking it in passively, like a stone takes in the moonlight. It had taken her months, years even, to become perfectly motionless, but she had done it: oh, yes, she had done it, and the Lady of Shadows had proclaimed her beautiful beyond measure, little mortal girl who saw no need to be quick, or hot, or restless.

But this world was made for quick, hot, restless things; not like the quiet Halls of the Dead. With a sigh, Nancy abandoned her stillness and turned to open her suitcase. Then she froze again, this time out of shock and dismay. Her clothing—the diaphanous gowns and gauzy black shirts she had packed with such care—was gone, replaced by a welter of fabrics as colorful as the things strewn on Sumi's side of the room. There was an envelope on top of the pile. With shaking fingers, Nancy picked it up and opened it.

Nancy—

We're sorry to play such a mean trick on you, sweetheart, but you didn't leave us much of a choice. You're going to boarding school to get better, not to keep wallowing in what your kidnappers did to you. We want our real daughter back. These clothes were your favorites before you disappeared. You used to be our little rainbow! Do you remember that?

You've forgotten so much.

We love you. Your father and I, we love you more than anything, and we believe you can come back to

*us. Please forgive us for packing you a more suitable
wardrobe, and know that we only did it because we
want the best for you. We want you back.*

*Have a wonderful time at school, and we'll be
waiting for you when you're ready to come home to
stay.*

The letter was signed in her mother's looping, unsteady
hand. Nancy barely saw it. Her eyes filled with hot, hate-
ful tears, and her hands were shaking, fingers cramping
until they had crumpled the paper into an unreadable
labyrinth of creases and folds. She sank to the floor, sitting
with her knees bent to her chest and her eyes fixed on the
open suitcase. How could she wear any of those things?
Those were *daylight* colors, meant for people who moved
in the sun, who were hot, and fast, and unwelcome in the
Halls of the Dead.

"What are you doing?" The voice belonged to Sumi.

Nancy didn't turn. Her body was already betraying her
by moving without her consent. The least she could do was
refuse to move it voluntarily.

"It *looks* like you're sitting on the floor and crying, which
everyone knows is dangerous, dangerous, don't-do-that
dangerous; it makes it look like you're not holding it together, and you might shake apart altogether," said Sumi.
She leaned close, so close that Nancy felt one of the other
girl's pigtails brush her shoulder. "Why are you crying,
ghostie girl? Did someone walk across your grave?"

"I never died, I just went to serve the Lord of the Dead

for a while, that's all, and I was going to stay forever, until he said I had to come back here long enough to be *sure*. Well, I was *sure* before I ever left, and I don't know why my door isn't here." The tears clinging to her cheeks were too hot. They felt like they were scalding her. Nancy allowed herself to move, reaching up and wiping them viciously away. "I'm crying because I'm angry, and I'm sad, and I want to go *home*."

"Stupid girl," said Sumi. She placed a sympathetic hand atop Nancy's head before smacking her—lightly, but still a hit—and leaping up onto her bed, crouching next to the open suitcase. "You don't mean home where your parents are, do you? Home to school and class and boys and blather, no, no, no, not for you anymore, all those things are for other people, people who aren't as special as you are. You mean the home where the man who bleached your hair lives. Or doesn't live, since you're a ghostie girl. A stupid ghostie girl. You can't go back. You have to know that by now."

Nancy raised her head and frowned at Sumi. "Why? Before I went through that doorway, I knew there was no such thing as a portal to another world. Now I know that if you open the right door at the right time, you might finally find a place where you belong. Why does that mean I can't go back? Maybe I'm just not finished being *sure*."

The Lord of the Dead wouldn't have lied to her, he *wouldn't*. He loved her.

He did.

"Because hope is a knife that can cut through the foundations of the world," said Sumi. Her voice was suddenly crystalline and clear, with none of her prior whimsy. She looked at Nancy with calm, steady eyes. "Hope *hurts*. That's what you need to learn, and fast, if you don't want it to cut you open from the inside out. Hope is bad. Hope means you keep on holding to things that won't ever be so again, and so you bleed an inch at a time until there's nothing left. Ely-Eleanor is always saying 'don't use this word' and 'don't use that word,' but she never bans the ones that are really *bad*. She never bans hope."

"I just want to go home," whispered Nancy.

"Silly ghost. That's all any of us want. That's why we're here," said Sumi. She turned to Nancy's suitcase and began poking through the clothes. "These are pretty. Too small for me. Why do you have to be so *narrow*? I can't steal things that won't fit, that would be silly, and I'm not getting any smaller here. No one ever does in this world. High Logic is no fun at all."

"I hate them," said Nancy. "Take them all. Cut them up and make streamers for your tree, I don't care, just get them away from me."

"Because they're the wrong colors, right? Somebody else's rainbow." Sumi bounced off the bed, slamming the suitcase shut and hauling it after her. "Get up, come on. We're going visiting."

"What?" Nancy looked after Sumi, bewildered and beaten down. "I'm sorry. I've just met you, and I really don't want to go anywhere with you."

"Then it's a good thing I don't care, isn't it?" Sumi beamed for a moment, bright as the hated, hated sun, and then she was gone, trotting out the door with Nancy's suitcase and all of Nancy's clothes.

Nancy didn't *want* those clothes, and for one tempting moment, she considered staying where she was. Then she sighed, and stood, and followed. She had little enough to cling to in this world. And she was eventually going to need clean underpants.

2 BEAUTIFUL BOYS AND GLAMOROUS GIRLS

SUMI WAS RESTLESS, in the way of the living, but even for the living, she was *fast*. She was halfway down the hall by the time Nancy emerged from the room. At the sound of Nancy's footsteps, she paused, looking back over her shoulder and scowling at the taller girl.

"Hurry, hurry, hurry," she scolded. "If dinner catches us without doing what needs done, we'll miss the scones and jam."

"Dinner *chases* you? And you have scones and jam for dinner if it doesn't catch you?" asked Nancy, bewildered.

"Not usually," said Sumi. "Not *often*. Okay, not ever, yet. But it could happen, if we wait long enough, and I don't want to miss out when it does! Dinners are mostly dull, awful things, all meat and potatoes and things to build healthy minds and bodies. *Boring.* I bet your dinners with the dead people were a lot more fun."

"Sometimes," admitted Nancy. There had been banquets, yes, feasts that lasted weeks, with the tables groaning under the weight of fruits and wines and dark, rich desserts. She had tasted unicorn at one of those feasts, and gone to her bed with a mouth that still tingled from the delicate venom of the horse-like creature's sweetened flesh. But mostly, there had been the silver cups of pomegranate juice, and the feeling of an empty stomach adding weight to her stillness. Hunger had died quickly in the Underworld. It was unnecessary, and a small price to pay for the quiet, and the peace, and the dances; for everything she'd so fervently enjoyed.

"See? Then you understand the importance of a good dinner," Sumi started walking again, keeping her steps short in deference to Nancy's slower stride. "Kade will get you fixed right up, right as rain, right as rabbits, you'll see. Kade knows where the best things are."

"Who is Kade? Please, you have to slow down." Nancy felt like she was running for her life as she tried to keep up with Sumi. The smaller girl's motions were too fast, too constant for Nancy's Underworld-adapted eyes to track them properly. It was like following a large hummingbird toward some unknown destination, and she was already exhausted.

"Kade has been here a very-very long time. Kade's parents don't want him back." Sumi looked over her shoulder and twinkled at Nancy. There was no other word to describe her expression, which was a strange combination of wrinkling her nose and tightening the skin around her eyes, all without visibly smiling. "My parents didn't want me back either, not unless I was willing to be their good little girl again and put all this nonsense about Nonsense aside. They sent me here, and then they died, and now they'll never want me at all. I'm going to live here always, until Ely-Eleanor has to let me have the attic for my own. I'll pull taffy in the rafters and give riddles to all the new girls."

They had reached a flight of stairs. Sumi began bounding up them. Nancy followed more sedately.

"Wouldn't you get spiders and splinters and stuff in the candy?" she asked.

Sumi rewarded her with a burst of laughter and an actual smile. "*Spi*ders and *splin*ters and *stuff*!" she crowed. "You're alliterating already! Oh, maybe we *will* be friends, ghostie girl, and this won't be completely dreadful after all. Now come on. We've much to do, and time does insist on being linear here, because it's awful."

The flight of stairs ended with a landing and another flight of stairs, which Sumi promptly started up, leaving Nancy no choice but to follow. All those days of stillness had made her muscles strong, accustomed to supporting her weight for hours at a time. Some people thought only motion bred strength. Those people were wrong. The mountain was as powerful as the tide, just . . . in a different way. Nancy *felt* like a mountain as she chased Sumi higher and higher into the house, until her heart was thundering in her chest and her breath was catching in her throat, until she feared that she would choke on it.

Sumi stopped in front of a plain white door marked only with a small, almost polite sign reading KEEP OUT. Grinning, she said, "If he meant that, he wouldn't say it. He knows that for anyone who's spent any time at all in Nonsense that, really, he's issuing an invitation."

"Why do people around here keep using that word like it's a place?" asked Nancy. She was starting to feel like she'd missed some essential introductory session about the school, one that would have answered all her questions and left her a little less lost.

"Because it is, and it isn't, and it doesn't matter," said Sumi, and knocked on the attic door before hollering, "We're coming in!" and shoving it open to reveal what looked like a cross between a used bookstore and a tailor's shop. Piles of books covered every available surface. The furniture, such as it was—a bed, a desk, a table—appeared to be made *from* the piles of books, all save for the bookshelves lining the walls. Those, at least, were made of wood, probably for the sake of stability. Bolts of fabric were piled atop the books. They ranged from cotton and muslin to velvet and the finest of thin, shimmering silks. At the center of it all, cross-legged atop a pedestal of paperbacks, sat the most beautiful boy Nancy had ever seen.

His skin was golden tan, his hair was black, and when he looked up—with evident irritation—from the book he was holding, she saw that his eyes were brown and his features were perfect. There was something timeless about him, like he could have stepped out of a painting and into the material world. Then he spoke.

"What'n the fuck are you doing in here again, Sumi?" he demanded, Oklahoma accent thick as peanut butter spread across a slice of toast. "I told you that you weren't welcome after the last time."

"You're just mad because I came up with a better filing system for your books than you could," said Sumi, sounding unruffled. "Anyway, you didn't mean it. I am the sunshine in your sky, and you'd miss me if I was gone."

"You organized them by color, and it took me weeks to figure out where anything was. I'm doing important research up here." Kade unfolded his legs and slid down from his pile of books. He knocked off a paperback in the process, catching it deftly before it could hit the ground. Then he turned to look at Nancy. "You're new. I hope she's not already leading you astray."

"So far, she's just led me to the attic," said Nancy inanely. Her cheeks reddened, and she said, "I mean, no. I'm not so easy to lead places, most of the time."

"She's more of a 'standing really still and hoping nothing eats her' sort of girl," said Sumi, and thrust the suitcase toward him. "Look what her parents did."

Kade raised his eyebrows as he took in the virulent pinkness of the plastic. "That's colorful," he said after a moment. "Paint could fix it."

"Outside, maybe. You can't paint underpants. Well, you *can*, but then they come out all stiff, and no one believes you didn't mess them." Sumi's expression sobered for a moment. When she spoke again, it was with a degree of clarity that was almost unnerving, coming from her. "Her parents swapped out her things before they sent her off to school. They knew she wouldn't like it, and they did it anyway. There was a note."

"Oh," said Kade, with sudden understanding. "One of those. All right. Is this going to be a straight exchange, then?"

"I'm sorry, I don't understand what's going on," said Nancy. "Sumi grabbed my suitcase and ran away with it. I don't want to bother anyone. . . ."

"You're not bothering me," said Kade. He took the suitcase from Sumi before turning toward Nancy. "Parents don't always like to admit that things have changed. They want the world to be exactly the way it was before their children went away on these life-changing adventures, and when the world doesn't oblige, they try to force it into the boxes they build for us. I'm Kade, by the way. Fairyland."

"I'm Nancy, and I'm sorry, I don't understand."

"I went to a Fairyland. I spent three years there, chasing rainbows and growing up by inches. I killed a Goblin King with his own sword, and he made me his heir with his dying breath, the Goblin Prince in Waiting." Kade walked off into the maze of books, still carrying Nancy's suitcase. His voice drifted back, betraying his location. "The King was my enemy, but he was the first adult to see me clearly in my entire life. The court of the Rainbow Princess was shocked, and they threw me down the next wishing well we passed. I woke up in a field in the middle of

Nebraska, back in my ten-year-old body, wearing the dress I'd had on when I first fell into the Prism." The way he said "Prism" left no question about what he meant: it was a proper name, the title of some strange passage, and his voice ached around that single syllable like flesh aches around a knife.

"I still don't understand," said Nancy.

Sumi sighed extravagantly. "He's *saying* he fell into a Fairyland, which is sort of like going to a Mirror, only they're really high Logic pretending to be high Nonsense, it's *quite* unfair, there's rules on rules on rules, and if you break one, wham"—she made a slicing gesture across her throat—"out you go, like last year's garbage. *They* thought they had snicker-snatched a little girl—fairies love taking little girls, it's like an addiction with them—and when they found out they had a little boy who just *looked* like a little girl on the outside, uh-oh, donesies. They threw him right back."

"Oh," said Nancy.

"Yeah," said Kade, emerging from the maze of books. He wasn't carrying Nancy's suitcase anymore. Instead, he had a wicker basket filled with fabric in reassuring shades of black and white and gray. "We had a girl here a few years ago who'd spent basically a decade living in a Hammer film. Black and white everything, flowy, lacy, super-Victorian. Seems like your style. I think I've guessed your size right, but if not, feel free to come and let me know that you need something bigger or smaller. I didn't take you for the corsetry type. Was I wrong?"

"What? Um." Nancy wrenched her gaze away from the basket. "No. Not really. The boning gets uncomfortable after a day or two. We were more, um, Grecian where I was, I guess. Or Pre-Raphaelite." She was lying, of course: she knew exactly what the styles had been in her Underworld, in those sweet and silent halls. When she'd gone looking for signs that someone else knew where to find a door, combing through Google and chasing links across Wikipedia, she had come across the works of a painter named Waterhouse, and she'd cried from the sheer relief of seeing people wearing clothes that didn't offend her eyes.

Kade nodded, understanding in his expression. "I manage the clothing swaps and inventory the wardrobes, but I do custom jobs too," he said. "You'll have to pay for those, since they're a lot more work on my part. I take information as well as cash. You could tell me about your door and where you went, and I could make you a few things that might fit you better."

Nancy's cheeks reddened. "I'd like that," she said.

"Cool. Now get out, both of you. We have dinner in a little while, and I want to finish my book." Kade's smile was fleeting. "I never did like to leave a story unfinished."

SUMI WATCHED NANCY as they walked down the stairs. The taller girl was holding tight to her basket of black and white clothing, cheeks still faintly touched with red. The color seemed almost obscene on her, like it had no business there.

"Do you want to fuck him?"

Nancy almost fell down the stairs.

After she had caught herself on the banister, she turned to Sumi, sputtering and blushing, and said, "*No!*"

"Are you sure? Because you looked like you did, and then you looked sort of upset, like you'd figured out you didn't want to after all. Jill—you'll meet her at dinner—wanted to fuck him until she found out he used to be a girl, and then she called him 'she' until Miss Ely said that we respect people's personal identities here, and then we all had to listen to this weird story about a girl who used to live in the attic who was really a rainbow who'd managed to offend the King of the Sky in one of the Fairylands and got herself kicked out." Sumi paused to take a breath and added, "That was sort of scary. You never think about people from *there* winding up *here,* only people from *here* winding up *there.* Maybe the walls are never as impermeable as we think they are."

"Yes," said Nancy, recovering her composure. She began walking again. "I'm quite sure I don't want to . . . have sexual relations with him, and I don't think his gender expression is any of my business." She was reasonably sure that was the right way to say things. She'd known the words once, before she left this world, and its problems, behind her. "That's between him and whoever he does, or doesn't, decide to get involved with."

"If you don't want to do the bing-bang with Kade, I guess I should tell you I'm taken," said Sumi breezily. "He's a candy corn farmer from the far reaches of the Kingdom and my one true love, and we're going to get married someday. Or we would have, if I hadn't gone and gotten myself exiled. Now he'll tend his fields alone, and I'll grow up and decide that he was just a dream, and maybe one day my daughter's daughter will visit his grave with licorice flowers and a prayer for the departed on her lips."

Her tone never wavered, not even as she was talking about the death of someone she called her one true love. Nancy gave her a sidelong look, trying to decide how serious she was. It was difficult to tell with Sumi.

They had reached the door to their shared room. Nancy reached a decision at the same time. "It doesn't matter whether you're taken or not," she said, opening the door and walking toward her bed. She put down the basket of clothing. She would need to go through it at more length, to check the fits and fabrics, but it was already an improvement over what she had left behind with Kade. "I don't do that. With anyone."

"You're celibate?"

"No. Celibacy is a choice. I'm asexual. I don't get those feelings." She would have thought her lack of sexual desire had been what had drawn her to the Underworld—so many people had called her a "cold fish" and said she was dead inside back when she'd been attending an ordinary high school, among ordinary teenagers, after all—except that none of the people she'd met in those gloriously haunted halls had shared her orientation. They lusted as hotly as the living did. The Lord of the Dead and the Lady of Shadows had spread their ardor throughout the palace, and all had been warmed by its light. Nancy smiled a little at the memory, until she realized Sumi was still watching her. She shook her head. "I just . . . I just don't. I can appreciate how beautiful someone is, and I can be attracted to them romantically, but that's as far as it goes with me."

"Huh," said Sumi, heading for her own side of the room. Then: "Well, okay. Is it going to bother you if I masturbate?"

"What, right *now*?" Nancy was unable to keep the horror from her voice. Not at the thought of masturbation— at the idea that this girl she had just met was going to drop her trousers and go to town.

"Um, ew," said Sumi, wrinkling her nose. "No, I meant in general. Like, late at night, when the lights are low and the moon-mantas are spreading their wings across the sky, and a girl's fingers might get the urge to go plowing in the fields."

"Please stop," said Nancy weakly. "No, I will not be upset if you masturbate. At night. In the dark. Without telling me about it. I have nothing against masturbation. I just don't want to watch."

"Neither did my last roommate," said Sumi, and that seemed to be the end of that, at least as far as she was concerned; she climbed out the window, leaving Nancy alone with her thoughts, the room, and her new wardrobe.

Nancy watched the empty window for almost a minute before she sank onto the bed and put her head in her hands. She'd expected boarding to school to be full of people like her, quiet and serious and eager to go back to the lands they'd left. Not . . . this. Not Sumi, and people slinging around technical terms for things she didn't understand.

She felt like she was trying to sail her way home without a map. She'd been sent back to the world of her birth to be *sure* . . . and she'd never been less sure in her life.

DINNER WAS HELD in the downstairs ballroom, a single, vast space made even larger by the polished marble floor and the vaulted cathedral ceiling. Nancy paused in the doorway, daunted by the scope of it, and by the sight of her classmates, who dotted the tables like so many knickknacks. There were seats for a hundred students, maybe more, but there were only forty or so in the room. They were so small, and the space was so big.

"It's rude and lewd to block the *food*," said Sumi, shoving past her. Nancy was knocked off balance and stumbled over the threshold into the ballroom. Silence fell as everyone turned to look at her. Nancy froze. It was the only defense mechanism she had learned from her time among the dead. When she was still, the ghosts couldn't see her to steal her life away. Stillness was the ultimate protection.

A hand settled on her shoulder. "Ah, Nancy, good," said Eleanor. "I was hoping I'd run into you before you reached a table. Be a good girl and escort an old woman to her seat."

Nancy turned her head. Eleanor had changed for dinner, trading electric orange trousers and rainbow sweater for a lovely sheath dress made from tie-dyed muslin. It was shockingly bright. Much like the sun, it hurt Nancy's eyes.

Still, she offered her arm to the older woman, unable to think of anything else that would fit the laws of propriety.

"How are you and Sumi getting on?" asked Eleanor, as they walked toward the tables.

"She's very . . . abrupt," said Nancy.

"She lived in high Nonsense for almost ten years subjective time, and much as you learned to be still, she learned never to stop," said Eleanor. "Stopping is what got people killed where she was. It was very close to where I was, you see, so I understand her better than most. She's a good girl. She won't steer you wrong."

"She took me to meet a boy named Kade," said Nancy.

"Oh? It's unusual for her to start making introductions that quickly—unless . . . Did you have trouble with your clothing? Was what you packed not what you found in your suitcase?"

Nancy didn't say anything. Her reddening cheeks and averted eyes said it all. Eleanor sighed.

"I'll write your parents and remind them that they agreed to allow me to guide your therapy. We should be able to have whatever they removed from your suitcase mailed here within the month. In the meantime, you can go back to Kade for whatever you need. The dear boy is a whiz with a needle. I really don't know how we got along without him."

"Sumi said he'd been to something called a 'high Logic world'? I still don't understand what any of those words mean. You throw them around like everyone knows them, but they're all new to me."

"I know, dear. You'll have therapy tonight and a proper orientation with Lundy tomorrow, and she'll explain everything." Eleanor straightened as they reached the tables, taking her hand from Nancy's arm. She clapped, twice. All conversation stopped. The students seated there—most with spaces between them, a few in tight conversational knots that left no visible way in—turned to look at her, faces expectant.

"Good evening, everyone," said Eleanor. "By now, some of you have doubtlessly heard that we have a new student with us. This is Nancy. She'll be rooming with Sumi until one of them attempts to murder the other. If you'd like to place a bet on who kills who, please talk to Kade."

Laughter from the girls—and they were *overwhelmingly* girls, Nancy realized. Apart from Kade, who was sitting by himself with his nose buried in a book, there were only three boys in the entire group. It seemed odd for a coed school to be so unbalanced. She didn't say anything. Eleanor had promised her an orientation, and maybe everything would be explained there, making questions unnecessary.

"Nancy is still adjusting to being back in this world after her travels, so please be gentle with her for the first few days, even as all of us were gentle with you, once upon a time." There was a thin line of steel in Eleanor's words. "When she's ready to join in with the hurly-burly and the cheerful malice, she'll let you know. Now, eat up, all of you, even though you may not want to. We are in a material place. Blood flows in your veins. Try to keep it there." She stepped away from Nancy, leaving her anchorless as she walked away.

Dinner was set up buffet-style along one wall. Nancy drifted over to it, recoiling from the braising dishes of meat and baked vegetables. They would sit like stones in her stomach, too heavy and unforgiving to tolerate. In the end, she filled a plate with grapes, slices of melon, and a scoop of cottage cheese. Picking up a glass of cranberry juice, she turned to consider the tables.

She'd been good at this, once. She'd never been one of the most popular girls in her high school, but she'd understood the game enough to play it, and play it well, to read the temperature of a room and find the safe shallows, where the currents of mean-girl intensity wouldn't wash her away, but where she wouldn't risk drowning in the brackish tide pools of the outcasts and the unwanted. She remembered a time when it had mattered so *much*. Sometimes she wished she knew how to get back to the girl who'd cared about such things. Other times, she was grateful beyond words that she couldn't.

The boys, except for Kade, were all sitting together, blowing bubbles in their milk and laughing. No; not them. One group had formed around a girl who was so dazzlingly beautiful that Nancy's eyes refused to focus on her face; another had formed around a punch bowl filled with candy-pink liquid from which they all furtively sipped. Neither looked welcoming. Nancy looked around until she found the only safe harbor she was likely to see, and started in that direction.

Sumi was sitting across from a pair of girls who couldn't have looked more different—or more alike. Her plate was piled high with no concern for what touched what. Gravy-covered melon slices cascaded into roast beef coated in jam. The sight of it made Nancy's stomach flip, but she still put her plate down next to Sumi's, cleared her throat, and asked the ritual question:

"Is this seat taken?"

"Sumi was just explaining how you're the most boring cardboard parody of a girl ever to walk this world or any other, and we should all feel sorry for you," said one of the strangers, adjusting her glasses as she turned to look at Nancy. "That makes you sound like my kind of person. Please, sit, and relieve some of the tedium of our table."

"Thank you," said Nancy, and settled.

The strangers wore the same face in remarkably different ways. It was amazing how a little eyeliner and a downcast expression, or a pair of wire-framed glasses and a steely gaze could transform what should have been identical into something distinct and individual. They both had long blonde hair, freckles across the bridges of their noses, and narrow shoulders. One was dressed in a white button-down shirt, jeans, and a black vest that managed to come across as old-fashioned and fashion-forward at the same time; her hair was tied back, no-nonsense and no frills. Her only adornment was a bow tie patterned with tiny biohazard symbols. The other wore a flowing pink dress with a low-cut bodice and a truly astonishing number of lace flourishes. Her hair hung in loose curls the size of soup cans, gathered at the back with a single pink ribbon. A matching ribbon was tied around her neck, like a makeshift choker. Both appeared to be in their late teens, with eyes that were much older.

"I'm Jack, short for Jacqueline," said the one in the glasses. She pointed to the one in pink. "This is Jill, short for Jillian, because our parents should never have been allowed to name their own children. You're Nancy."

"Yes," said Nancy, unsure of how else she was expected to respond. "It's nice to meet you both."

Jill, who otherwise had neither moved nor spoken since Nancy approached the table, turned her eyes toward Nancy's plate and said, "You aren't eating much. Are you on a diet?"

"No, not really. I just . . ." Nancy hesitated before shaking her head and saying, "My stomach's upset from the trip and the stress and everything."

"Am I the stress, or am I everything?" asked Sumi, picking up a jam-sticky piece of meat and popping it in her mouth. Around it, she continued, "I guess I could be both. I'm flexible."

"I'm on a diet," said Jill proudly. Her plate contained nothing but the rarest strips of roast, some of them so red and bloody that they were virtually raw. "I eat meat every other day and spinach the rest of the time. My blood is so iron-rich you could set a compass by it."

"That's, um, very nice," said Nancy, looking to Sumi for help. She'd known girls on diets her entire life. Iron-rich blood had rarely, if ever, been their goal. Most of them had been looking for smaller waists, clearer complexions, and richer boyfriends, spurred on by a deeply ingrained self-loathing that had been manufactured for them before they were old enough to understand the kind of quicksand they were sinking in.

Sumi swallowed. "Jack and Jill went up the hill, to watch a bit of slaughter, Jack fell down and broke her crown, and Jill came tumbling after."

Jack looked long-suffering. "I hate that rhyme."

"And that's not what happened at all," said Jill. She turned to beam at Nancy. "We went to a very nice place, where we met very nice people who loved us very much. But there was a little problem with the local constabulary, and we had to come back to this world for a while, for our own safety."

"What have I told you about abusing the word 'very'?" asked Jack. She sounded tired.

"Jack and Jill are more stupid, stupid girls," said Sumi. She stabbed a slice of melon with her fork, splashing gravy on the table. "They think they're going *back,* but they're *not.* Those doors are closed now. Can't go high Logic, high Wicked if you're not innocent. The Wicked doesn't want people it can't *spoil.*"

"I don't understand anything you people say," said Nancy. "Logic? Nonsense? Wicked? What do those things even *mean*?"

"They're directions, or the next best thing," said Jack. She leaned forward, dragging her index finger through the wet ring left by the base of a glass and using the moisture to draw a cross on the table. "Here in the so-called 'real

world,' you have north, south, east, and west, right? Those
don't work for most of the portal worlds we've been able to
catalog. So we use other words. Nonsense, Logic, Wickedness, and Virtue. There are smaller subdirections, little
branches that may or may not go anywhere, but those four
are the big ones. Most worlds are either high Nonsense *or*
high Logic, and then they have some degree of Wickedness
or Virtue built into their foundations from there. A sur-
prising number of Nonsense worlds are Virtuous. It's like
they can't work up the attention span necessary for anything more vicious than a little mild naughtiness."

Jill gave Nancy a sidelong look. "Did that help at all?"

"Not really," said Nancy. "I never thought that . . . You
know, I read *Alice's Adventures in Wonderland* when I was
a kid, and I never thought about what it would be like for
Alice when she went back to where she'd started. I figured
she'd just shrug and get over it. But I can't do that. Every
time I close my eyes, I'm back in my real bed, in my real
room, and all of this is the dream."

"It isn't home anymore, is it?" asked Jill gently. Nancy
shook her head, blinking back tears. Jill reached across the
table to pat her hand. "It gets better. It never gets easy, but
it does start to hurt a little less. How long has it been for
you?"

"Just under two months." Seven weeks, four days since
the Lord of the Dead had told her she needed to be *sure*.
Seven weeks, four days since the door to her chambers had
opened on the basement she'd left behind so long before,
in the house she thought she'd left behind forever. Seven

weeks, four days since her screaming had alerted her parents to an intruder and they had come pounding down the steps, only to sweep her into an unwanted embrace, bawling about how upset they'd been when she had disappeared.

She'd been gone for six months, from their perspective. One month for each of the pomegranate seeds that Persephone had eaten, back at the beginning of things. Years for her, and months for them. They still thought she was dyeing her hair. They still thought she was eventually going to tell them where she'd been.

They still thought a lot of things.

"It gets better," repeated Jill. "It's been a year and a half, for us. But we don't lose hope. I keep my iron levels up. Jack has her experiments—"

Jack didn't say anything. She just stood and walked away from the table, leaving her half-eaten dinner behind.

"We're not cleaning up after you!" shouted Sumi, around a mouthful of food.

In the end, of course, they did. There was really no other option.

3 BIRDS OF A FEATHER

ACCORDING TO WHAT Nancy's parents had told her about the school, the mandatory group therapy had been one of the big selling points. What better way to bring their teenage daughter back from whatever strange hole she'd crawled into than having her sit and talk to people who'd suffered similar traumas, all under the watchful eye of a trained professional? As she sank into the embrace of a thickly padded armchair, surrounded by teens who twitched, chewed their hair, or stared moodily off into space without speaking, she had to wonder what they would have thought of the reality.

Then the eight-year-old walked into the room.

She was dressed like a middle-aged librarian, wearing a pencil skirt and a white blouse, both of which were much too old for her. Her hair was pulled back into a tight,

no-nonsense bun. The overall effect was of a child playing dress-up in her mother's closet. Nancy sat up straighter.
The school's brochures had mentioned an age range of
twelve to nineteen, allowing both the precocious and those
who needed a little time to catch up to attend. It hadn't said
anything about children under the age of ten.

The girl stopped at the center of the room, turning to
look at each of them in turn. One by one, the fidgeters became still; the hair chewers stopped chewing; even Sumi,
who'd been doing an elaborate cat's-cradle with a piece of
yarn, lowered her hands and sat quietly. The girl smiled.

"For those of you who've been here for a while, welcome
to Wednesday night group. We're going to be sharing with
the high Wicked visitors tonight, but as always, the discus-
sion is open to all." Her voice matched her body. Her tone
was older, cadenced like an adult woman's, rendered high
and strange by her prepubescent vocal cords. She looked
at Nancy as she continued. "For those of you who are new
here, my name is Lundy, and I am a fully licensed therapist with a specialization in child psychology. I'm going to
be helping you through your recovery process."

Nancy stared. She couldn't think of anything else to do.

As Lundy walked over to the one remaining chair, Kade
leaned over and murmured, "She's one of us, only she went
to a high Logic, high Wicked world where they kicked visitors out on their eighteenth birthdays. She didn't want to
leave, so she asked one of the local apothecaries to help her.
This was the result. Eternal childhood."

"Not eternal, Mr. Bronson," said Lundy sharply. Kade

sat up and settled back in his own chair, shrugging un-apologetically. Lundy sighed. "You would have gotten this at your orientation, Miss, ah . . . ?"

"Whitman," said Nancy.

"Miss Whitman," said Lundy. "As I was saying, you would have gotten this at your orientation, but: I'm not living out an eternal childhood. I'm aging in reverse, grow-ing one week younger for every month that passes. I'll live a long, long time. Longer, maybe, than I would have had I continued aging in the usual way. But they threw me out anyway, because I had broken the rules. I'll never marry, or have a family of my own, and my daughters will never find their way to the door that once led me to the Goblin Mar-ket. So I suppose I've learnt the danger of making impor-tune bargains with the fae, and can now serve as a warning to others. I am still, however, your therapist. It's amazing, the degrees you can get over the Internet these days."

"I'm sorry," whispered Nancy.

Lundy waved a hand as she sat, dismissing Nancy's apol-ogy. "It's no matter, honestly. Everyone finds out eventu-ally. Now. Who wants to share first?"

Nancy sat in silence as the other students talked. Not all of them: slightly less than half seemed to have been to a world that fell on the "Wicked" side of the compass, or maybe that was just the number who felt like sharing. Jill recited an impassioned paean to the moors and wind-racked hills of the world she'd gone to with her sister, while Jack only muttered something about burning windmills and the importance of fire safety in laboratory settings.

A girl with hair the color of moonlight on wheat stared at her hands while she talked about boys made of glass whose kisses had cut her lips but whose hearts had been kind and true. The girl who was too beautiful to look at directly said something about Helen of Troy, and half the room laughed, but not because it was funny; because she was so beautiful that they wanted nothing more than they wanted her to like them.

Kade made a brief, bitter speech about how Wickedness and Virtue were just labels and didn't mean anything; the world he'd been to was labeled "Virtue" on all the maps, but it had still cast him out as soon as it realized what he was.

Finally, silence fell, and Nancy realized everyone was looking at her. She shrank back in her seat. "I don't know if the place I went was wicked or not," she said. "It never seemed wicked to me. It always seemed . . . kind, at the root of things. Yes, there were rules, and yes, there were punishments if you broke them, but they were never unfair, and the Lord of the Dead took good care of everyone who served in his halls. I don't think it was wicked at all."

"How can you be sure, though?" asked Sumi, and her voice was gentle, underneath her jeering tone. "You can't even say Wicked right. Maybe it was evil to the core, filled with wiggling worms and bad stuff, and you couldn't see it." She slanted a glance toward Jill, almost as if she were checking the other girl's reaction. Jill, whose eyes were fixed on Nancy, didn't appear to notice. "You shouldn't close doors just because you don't like what's on the other side."

"I know because I know," said Nancy doggedly. "I didn't go anyplace bad. I went *home*."

"That's the thing people forget when they start talking about things in terms of good and evil," said Jack, turning to look at Lundy. She adjusted her glasses as she continued, "For us, the places we went were home. We didn't care if they were good or evil or neutral or what. We cared about the fact that for the first time, we didn't have to pretend to be something we weren't. We just got to *be*. That made all the difference in the world."

"And on that note, I suppose we're done for the evening." Lundy stood. Nancy realized with a start that somewhere in the middle of the session, she'd started thinking of the little girl as an adult woman. It was the way she carried herself: too mature for the body she inhabited, too weary for the face she wore. "Thank you, everyone. Miss Whitman, I'll see you tomorrow morning for orientation. Everyone else, I'll see you tomorrow evening, when we'll be speaking to those who have traveled to the high Logic worlds. Remember, only by learning about the journeys of others can we truly understand our own."

"Oh, lovely," muttered Jack. "I do so love being in the hot seat two nights running."

Lundy ignored her, walking calmly out of the room. As soon as she was gone, Eleanor appeared in the doorway, all smiles.

"All right, my crumpets, it's time for good little girls and boys to go to bed," she said, and clapped her hands. "Off you go. Dream sweetly, try not to sleepwalk, and please don't wake me up at midnight trying to force a portal to manifest in the downstairs pantry. It isn't going to happen."

The students rose and scattered, some moving off in pairs, others going alone. Sumi went out the window, and no one commented on her disappearance.

Nancy walked back to her room, pleased to find it bathed in moonlight and filled with silence. She disrobed, garbed herself in a white nightgown from the pile Kade had given her, and stretched out on her bed, lying atop the covers. She closed her eyes, slowed her breathing, and slipped into sweet, motionless sleep, her first day done, and her future yet ahead of her.

ORIENTATION WITH LUNDY the next morning was odd, to say the least. It was held in a small room that had been a study once, before it had been filled with blackboards and the smell of chalk dust. Lundy stood at the center of it all, one hand resting on a wheeled stepladder, which she moved from blackboard to blackboard as the need to climb up and point to some complicated diagram arose. The need seemed to arise with dismaying frequency. Nancy sat very still in the room's single chair, her head spinning as she struggled to keep up.

Lundy's explanation of the cardinal directions of portals had been, if anything, less helpful than Jack's, and had involved a lot more diagrams, and some offhanded comments about minor directions, like Whimsy and Wild. Nancy had bitten her tongue to keep from asking any questions. She was deeply afraid that Lundy would attempt to answer them, and then her head might actually explode.

Finally, Lundy stopped and looked expectantly at Nancy. "Well?" she asked. "Do you have any questions, Miss Whitman?"

About a million, and all of them wanted to be asked at once, even the ones she didn't want to ask at all. Nancy took a deep breath and started with what seemed to be the easiest: "Why are there so many more girls here than boys?"

"Because 'boys will be boys' is a self-fulfilling prophecy," said Lundy. "They're too loud, on the whole, to be easily misplaced or overlooked; when they disappear from the home, parents send search parties to dredge them out of swamps and drag them away from frog ponds. It's not innate. It's learned. But it protects them from the doors, keeps them safe at home. Call it irony, if you like, but we spend so much time waiting for our boys to stray that they never have the opportunity. We notice the silence of men. We depend upon the silence of women."

"Oh," said Nancy. It made sense, in its terrible way. Most of the boys she'd known were noisy creatures, encouraged to be so by their parents and friends. Even when they were naturally quiet, they forced themselves to be loud, to avoid censure and mockery. How many of them could have slipped through an old wardrobe or into a rabbit's den and simply disappeared without sending up a thousand alarms? They would have been found and dragged back home before they reached the first enchanted mirror or climbed the first forbidden tower.

"We've always been open to male students; we just don't get many."

"Everyone here . . . everyone seems to want to go back." Nancy paused, struggling with the question that was trying to form. Finally, she asked, "How is it that *everyone* wants to go back? I thought people who went through this sort of thing mostly just wanted to go back to their old lives and forget that they'd ever known anything else."

"This isn't the only school, of course," said Lundy. She smiled at Nancy's surprise. "What, you thought Miss West could sweep up every child who'd ever stumbled into a painting and discovered a magical world on the other side? It happens all over the world, you know. The language barriers alone would make it impossible, as would the expense. There are two schools in North America, this campus and our sister school in Maine. That's where the students who hated their travels go, to learn how to move on. How to forget."

"So we're here to do . . . what?" asked Nancy. "Learn how to dwell? Eleanor dresses like she's still living on the other side of the mirror. Sumi is . . ." She didn't have the words for what Sumi was. She stopped speaking.

"Sumi is a classic example of someone who embraced life in a high Nonsense world," said Lundy. "She can't be blamed for what it made of her, any more than you can be blamed for the way you seem to stop breathing when no one's looking at you. She's going to need a lot of work before she's ready to face the world outside again, and she has to want to do it. That's what determines which school is better for you: the wanting. You want to go back, and so you hold on to the habits you learned while you were traveling, because it's better than admitting the journey's over. We don't teach you how to dwell. We also don't teach you how to forget. We teach you how to move on."

There was one more question that needed to be asked, a question bigger and more painful than all the questions before it. Nancy closed her eyes for a moment, allowing herself to sink into stillness. Then she opened them and asked, "How many of us have gone back?"

Lundy sighed. "Every student I've given this orientation to has asked that question. The answer is, we don't know. Some people, like Eleanor—like me—go back over and over again before we wind up staying in one world or the other for good. Others only take one trip in their lives. If your parents choose to withdraw you, or if you choose to withdraw yourself, we'll have no way of knowing what becomes of you. I know of three students who have returned to the worlds they left behind. Two were high Logic, both Fairylands. The third was high Nonsense. An Underworld, like the one you visited—although not the same, I'm afraid. That one was accessed by walking through a special mirror, under the full moon. The girl we lost to that world was home for the holidays when the door opened for her a second time. Her mother broke the glass after she went through. We learned later that the mother had also been there—it was a generational portal—and had wanted to spare her daughter the pain of returning."

"Oh," said Nancy, in a very small voice.

"The chances are, Miss Whitman, that you'll live out your days in this world. You may tell people of your adventures, when they're more distant, and when speaking of them hurts somewhat less. Many of our graduates have found that sort of sharing to be both cathartic and lucrative. People do so love a good fantasy." Lundy's expression was sorrowful but kind, like that of a doctor delivering a terminal diagnosis. "I won't stand here and say the door is closed forever, because there's no way of being sure. But I *will* tell you the odds were against you going in the first place, and that those same odds are against you now. They say lightning never strikes twice. Well, you're far more likely to be struck repeatedly by lightning than you are to find a second door."

"Oh," said Nancy again.

"I'm sorry." Then Lundy smiled, ridiculously bright. "Welcome to school, Miss Whitman. We hope that we can make you better."

PART II

WITH YOUR LOOKING-GLASS EYES

4 LIGHTNING TO KISS THE SKY

THE BUILDING WAS BIGGER than its population, filled with empty rooms and silent spaces. But all of them felt like they harbored the ghosts of the students who had tried—and failed—to find their way back to the worlds that had rejected them, and so Nancy fled to the outside. She hated to rush, but the sun burnt so badly that she actually *ran* for the deepest copse of trees she could find, shielding her eyes with her arm. She flung herself into the welcome shade of the grove, blinking back tears brought on as much by the light as by her dismay. Setting her back to an ancient oak, she sank to the ground, buried her face against her knees, and settled into perfect stillness as she wept.

"It's hard, isn't it?" The voice belonged to Jill, soft and wistful and filled with painful understanding. Nancy raised her head. The gossamer blonde was perched on a tree root, her pale lavender gown arranged to drape just so around her slender frame, a parasol resting against her left shoulder and blocking the sun that filtered down through the branches. Her choker today was deep purple, the color of elderberry wine.

"I'm sorry," said Nancy, wiping away her tears with slow swipes of her hand. "I didn't know there was anyone here."

"It's the shadiest spot on the grounds. I'm impressed, actually. It took me *weeks* to find the place." Jill's smile was kind. "I wasn't trying to say you should leave. I just meant, well, it's hard being here, surrounded by all these people who went to their pastel dream worlds full of sunshine and rainbows. They don't understand us."

"Um," said Nancy, glancing at Jill's pastel gown.

Jill laughed. "I don't wear these because I want to remember where I've been. I wear them because the Master liked it when I dressed in pale colors. They showed the blood better. Isn't that why you wear white? Because your Master liked to see you that way?"

"I . . ." Nancy stopped. "He wasn't my master, he was my Lord, and my teacher, and he loved me. I wear black and white because color is reserved for the Lady of Shadows and her entourage. I'd like to join them someday, if I can prove myself, but until then, I'm supposed to serve as a statue, and statues should blend in. Standing out is for people who've earned it." She touched the pomegranate ribbon in her hair—and one piece of color she *had* earned—before asking, "You had a . . . master?"

"Yes." Jill's smile was bright enough to replace the

blocked-away sun. "He was good to me. Gave me treats and trinkets and told me I was beautiful, even when I wasn't feeling well. *Jack* spent all her time locked away with her precious doctor, learning things that weren't ladylike or appropriate in the least, but I stayed in the high towers with the Master, and he taught me so many beautiful things. So many beautiful, wonderful things."

"I'm sorry you wound up back here," said Nancy.

Jill's smile died. She flapped a hand like she was trying to wave Nancy's words away, and said, "This isn't forever. The Master wanted to be rid of Jack. She didn't deserve what we had. So he arranged things so a door would open back to our world, and I stumbled and fell through after her. He'll find a way to open a door back to me. You'll see." She stood, spinning her parasol. "Excuse me. I have to go." Then she turned, not waiting for Nancy to say good-bye, and walked briskly away.

"And that, children, is why sometimes we don't let the Addams twins out into the general population," said a voice. Nancy looked up. Kade, who was seated on one of the tree's higher branches, waved sardonically down at her. "Hello, Nancy out of Wonderland. If you were looking for a private place to cry, you chose poorly."

"I didn't think anyone would be out here," she said.

"Because back at home, the other kids were more likely to hide in their rooms than they were to go running for the outdoors, right?" Kade closed his book. "The trouble is, you're at a school for people who never learned how to make the logical choice. So we go running for the tallest trees and the deepest holes whenever we want to be alone, and since there's a limited number of those, we wind up spending a lot of time together. I take it from the crying that your orientation didn't go well. Let me guess. Lundy told you about lightning striking twice."

Nancy nodded. She didn't speak. She no longer trusted her voice.

"She has a point, if your world kicked you out."

"It didn't kick me out," protested Nancy. She could still speak, after all, when she really needed to. "I was sent back to learn something, that's all. I'm going back."

Kade looked at her sympathetically and didn't contradict her. "Prism is never taking me back," he said instead. "That's not a nonstarter, that's a never-gonna-happen. I violated their rules when I wasn't what they wanted me to be, and the people who run that particular circus are *very* picky about rules. But Eleanor went back a bunch of times. Her door's still open."

"How . . . I mean, why . . ." Nancy shook her head. "Why did she stop? If her door is still open, why is she *here*, with us, and not there, where she *belongs*?"

Kade swung his legs around so they were braced on the same side of the branch. Then he dropped down from the tree, landing easily in front of Nancy. He straightened, saying, "This was a long time ago, and her parents were still alive. She thought she could have it all, go back and forth, spend as much time as possible in her real home without breaking her father's heart. But she forgot that adults don't thrive in Nonsense, even when they're raised to it. Every time she came back *here,* she got a little older. Until one day she went back *there,* and it nearly broke her. Can you imagine what that must have been like? It would be like opening the door that was supposed to take you home and discovering you couldn't breathe the air anymore."

"That sounds horrible," said Nancy.

"I guess it was." Kade sank down to sit, cross-legged, across from her. "Of course, she'd already spent enough time in Nonsense for it to have changed her. It slowed her aging—that's probably why she was able to keep going for as long as she did. Jack checked the record books the last time we had an excursion to town, and she found out Eleanor was almost a hundred. I always figured she was in her sixties. I asked her about it, and you know what she told me?"

"What?" asked Nancy, fascinated and horrified at the same time. Had the Underworld changed more than just her hair? Was she going to stay the same, immortal and unchanging, while everything around her withered and died?

"She said she's just waiting to get senile, like her mother and father did, because once her mind slips enough, she'll be able to tolerate the Nonsense again. She's going to run this school until she forgets why she isn't going back, and then, when she *does* go back, she'll be able to stay." He shook his head. "I can't decide if it's genius or madness."

"Maybe it's a little bit of both," said Nancy. "I'd do any-thing to go home."

"Most of the students here would," said Kade bitterly.

Nancy hesitated before she said, "Lundy said there was a sister school for people who *didn't* want to go back. People who wanted to forget. Why are you enrolled here, instead of there? You might be happier."

"But you see, I don't want to forget," said Kade. "I'm the loophole kid. I want to remember Prism more than anything. The way the air tasted, and the way the music sounded. Everyone played these funky pipes there, even little kids. Lessons started when you were, like, two, and it was another way of communicating. You could have whole conversations without putting down your pipes. I grew *up* there, even if I wound up getting tossed out and forced to do it all over again. I figured out who I was there. I kissed a girl with hair the color of cabbages and eyes the color of moth-wings, and she kissed me back, and it was wonderful. Just because I wouldn't go back if you paid me, that doesn't mean I want to forget a *second* of what happened to me. I wouldn't be who I am if I hadn't gone to Prism."

"Oh," said Nancy. It made sense, of course, it was just an angle she hadn't considered. She shook her head. "This is all so much more complicated than I ever expected it to be."

"Tell me about it, princess." Kade stood, offering her his hand. "Come on. I'll walk you back to school."

Nancy hesitated before reaching up and taking the offered hand, letting Kade pull her to her feet. "All right," she said.

"You're pretty when you smile," said Kade as he led her out of the trees, back toward the main building. Nancy couldn't think of anything to say in response to that, and so she didn't say anything at all.

CORE CLASSES WERE SURPRISINGLY dull, taught as they were by an assortment of adults who drove in from the town, Lundy, and Miss Eleanor herself. Nancy got the distinct feeling that someone had a chart showing exactly what was required by the state and that they were all receiving the educational equivalent of a balanced meal.

The electives were slightly better, including music, art, and something called "A Traveler's History of the Great Compass," which Nancy guessed had something to do with the various portal worlds and their relations to one another. After hesitantly considering her options, she had signed up. Maybe something in the syllabus would tell her more about where her Underworld fell.

After reading the introductory chapters of her home-printed textbook, she was still confused. The most common directions were Nonsense, usually paired with Virtue, and Logic, usually paired with Wicked. Sumi's madhouse of a world was high Nonsense. Kade's Prism was high Logic. With those as her touchstones, Nancy had decided that her Underworld was likely to have been Logic; it had consistent rules and expected them to be followed. But she couldn't see why it should really be considered Wicked just because it was ruled by the Lord of the Dead. Virtue seemed more likely. Her first actual class was scheduled for two days' time. It was too long to wait. It was no time at all.

By the end of her first day, she was exhausted, and her head felt like it had been stuffed well beyond any reasonable capacity, spinning with both mundane things like math and history, and with the ever-increasing vocabulary needed to talk to her fellow students. One, a shy girl with brown braids and thick glasses, had confessed that *her* world was at the nexus of two minor compass directions, being high Rhyme and high Linearity. Nancy hadn't known what to say to that, and so she hadn't said anything at all. Increasingly, that felt like the safest option she had.

Sumi was sitting on her bed, braiding bits of bright ribbon into her hair, when Nancy slipped into the room. "Tired as a titmouse at a bacchanal, little ghostie?" she asked.

"I don't know what you mean, so I'm going to assume you want to be taken at face value," said Nancy. "Yes. I am very tired. I'm going to bed."

"Ely-Eleanor thought you might be tired," said Sumi. "New girls always are. She said you can skip group tonight, but you can't make a habit of it. Words are an important part of the healing process. Words, words, words." She wrinkled her nose. "She asked me to remember so many of them, and all in the order she gave, and all for *you*. You're not Nonsense at all, are you, ghostie? You wouldn't want so many words if you were."

"I'm sorry," said Nancy. "I never said I was from . . . a place like you went to visit."

"Assumptions will be the death of all, and you're better than most of the roommates she's tried to give me; I'll keep you," said Sumi wearily. She stood, walking toward the door. "Sleep well, ghostie. I'll see you in the morning."

"Wait!" Nancy hadn't intended to speak; the word had simply escaped her lips, like a runaway calf. The thought horrified her. Her stillness was eroding, and if she stayed in this dreadful, motile world too long, she would never be able to get it back again.

Sumi turned to face her, cocking her head. "What do you want *now*?"

"I just wanted to know—I mean, I was just wondering—how old are you?"

"Ah." Sumi turned again, finishing her walk toward the door. Then, facing into the hall, she said, "Older than I look, younger than I ought to be. My skin is a riddle not to be solved, and even letting go of everything I love won't offer me the answer. My window is closing, if that's what you're asking. Every day I wake up a little more linear, a little less lost, and one day I'll be one of the women who says 'I had the most charming dream,' and I'll mean it. Old enough to know what I'm losing in the process of being found. Is that what you wanted to know?"

"No," said Nancy.

"Too bad," said Sumi, and left the room. She closed the door behind herself.

Nancy undressed alone, letting her clothes fall to the floor, until she stood naked in front of the room's single silver mirror. The electric light was harsh against her skin. She flipped the switch, and smiled to see her reflection transmuted into the purest marble, becoming unyielding, unbending stone. She stood there, frozen, for almost an hour before she finally felt like she could sleep, and slid, still naked, between her sheets.

She woke to a room full of sunlight and the sound of screaming.

Screams had not been not uncommon in the Halls of the Dead. There was an art to decoding their meaning: screams of pleasure, screams of pain, screams of sheer boredom in the face of an uncaring eternity. These were screams of panic and fear. Nancy rolled out of her bed in an instant, grabbing her nightgown from where it lay discarded at the foot of the bed and yanking it on over her head. She didn't feel like running into potential danger while completely exposed. She didn't feel like *running* anywhere, but the screams were still happening, and it seemed like the appropriate thing to do.

Sumi's bed was empty. The thought that Sumi could be the screamer crossed Nancy's mind as she ran, but was quickly dismissed. Sumi was not a screamer. Sumi was a reason for *other* people to scream.

Half a dozen girls were clustered in the hallway, forming an unbreakable wall of flannel and silk. Nancy pushed her way into their midst and stopped, freezing in place. It was a stillness so absolute, so profound, that she would have been proud of herself under any other circumstances. As it was, this felt less like proper stillness and more like the freeze of a rabbit when faced with the promise of a snake.

Sumi was the cause of the screaming: that much was clear. She was slumped limply against the base of the wall, eyes closed. She wasn't breathing, and her hands—her clever, never-still hands—were gone, severed at the wrists. She would never tie another knot or weave another cat's cradle out of yarn. Someone had stolen that from her. Someone had stolen *everything* from her.

"Oh," whispered Nancy, and the sound was like a stone dropped into a still pool: small, but creating ripples that touched everything in their path. One of the girls whirled and ran, shouting for Miss Eleanor. Another began to sob, pressing her back to the wall and sinking down to the floor until she looked like a cruel parody of Sumi. Nancy thought about telling her to get up and decided against it. What did she know of grief in the face of death? All the dead people she'd ever met had been perfectly pleasant and not overly inconvenienced by the fact that they no longer had material bodies. Maybe Sumi would find her way to the Underworld and be able to tell the Lord of the Dead that Nancy was still trying to be sure, so that she could come back. He would be pleased, Nancy was sure, to hear that she was trying.

Belatedly, Nancy realized that it might look suspicious, her roommate dying when she had just arrived from the Underworld—maybe they would assume she preferred the dead to the living, or that Eleanor's comments about them killing each other had been warnings—but since she hadn't touched Sumi, she decided not to worry about it. There were better things to worry about, like Eleanor, now hurrying along the hall, flanked by the girl who'd run to fetch her on one side and by Lundy on the other. Lundy was wearing a grandmotherly flannel nightgown, with curlers in her hair. It should have looked ridiculous. Somehow, it just looked sad.

The girls parted to let Eleanor through. She stopped a few feet from Sumi, pressing one hand over her mouth, her eyes filling with tears. "Oh, my poor girl," she murmured, kneeling to press her fingers to the side of Sumi's neck. It was just a formality: she had clearly been dead for quite some time. "Who did this to you? Who could have done this to you?"

Nancy was somehow unsurprised when several of the girls turned to look at her. She was new; she had been touched by the dead. She didn't protest her innocence. She just held up her hands, showing them the pale, unblemished skin. There was no way she could have washed the blood away so completely in one of their shared bathrooms, not without being seen. Even in the middle of the night, the amount of scrubbing required to get the blood from under her fingernails would have attracted attention, and she would have been undone.

"Leave poor Nancy alone; she didn't do this," said Eleanor. She wiped her eyes before offering her arm to Lundy, who helped her up. "No daughter of the Underworld would kill someone who hadn't earned their place in those hallowed halls, isn't that right, Nancy? She might be a murderess someday, but not on the basis of two days' acquaintance." Her tone was leaden with sorrow but perfectly matter-of-fact at the same time, as if the idea that Nancy might someday start mowing her friends down like wheat was of no real concern.

In the here and now, Nancy supposed that it wasn't. She watched dully as Lundy produced a sheet from somewhere—linen closets, there had to be linen closets in a house this large—and covered Sumi's body. The blood from Sumi's stumps soaked through the fabric almost instantly, but it was still a little bit better than looking at the motionless girl with the ribbons in her hair.

"What happened?"

Nancy glanced to the side. Jack had appeared next to her, the collar of her shirt open and her bow tie hanging untied on the left. She looked unfinished. "If you don't know what happened, why are you here?" It occurred to Nancy that she didn't know where Jack's room was, and she amended, "Unless this is your hall."

"No, Jill and I sleep in the basement. It's more comfortable for us, all things considered." She adjusted her glasses, squinting at the red blotches on the sheet. "That's blood. Who's under the sheet?"

The girl with the brown braids from the Rhyme and Linearity world turned to glare at Jack. There was pure hatred in her gaze, enough that Nancy took an involuntary step backward. "Like you don't know, you *murderer*," she spat. "You did this, didn't you? This is just like what happened to Angela's guinea pig. You can't keep your hands or your scalpels to yourself."

"I told you, it was a cultural mix-up," said Jack. "The

guinea pig was in a common area, and I thought it was supposed to be for anyone who wanted it."

"It was a *pet*," snapped the girl.

Jack shrugged helplessly. "I offered to put it back together. Angela declined."

"New girl." The voice was Kade's. Nancy looked over to see him nodding toward her room. "Why don't you take that Addams and show her your room? I'll try to intercept the other one before she can show up and start trouble."

"Anything to avoid another angry mob with torches," said Jack, seizing Nancy's hand. "Show me your room."

It sounded like a command rather than a request. Nancy didn't argue. Under the circumstances, getting Jack out of sight and hence hopefully out of mind seemed much more important than forcing the other girl to ask nicely. She turned and hauled Jack to her door, still ajar after her hurried exit, and then inside.

Jack let go of Nancy's hand as soon as they were inside, producing a handkerchief from her pocket and wiping her fingers. Her cheeks reddened when she saw Nancy's startled look. "Difficult as it may be to believe, none of us escaped our travels unscathed, not even me," she said. "I am perhaps a bit *too* aware of the natural world and its many wonders. A lot of those wonders would like nothing more than to melt the skin off your body. All those people in their creepy labs hooking dead bodies up to funky wires? There's a reason they usually wear gloves."

"I don't really understand what the world you traveled to was *like*," said Nancy. "Sumi's world was all about candy and not making any sense at all, and Kade went to a war or something, but the world you describe and the world Jill describes barely seem to match up."

"That's because the worlds we experienced barely seemed to match up, despite being the same place," said Jack. "Our parents were . . . let's go with 'overbearing.' The sort who always wanted to put things in boxes. I think they hated us being identical twins more than we did."

"But your names—"

Jack shrugged broadly, tucking the handkerchief back into her pocket. "They weren't so upset that they were willing to pass up the chance to make our lives a living hell. Parents are special that way. For some reason, they'd expected fraternal twins, maybe even that holy grail of the instant nuclear family, a boy and a girl. Instead, they got us. Ever watch a pair of perfectionists try to decide which of their identical children is the 'smart one' versus the 'pretty one'? It would have been funny, if our lives hadn't been the prize they were trying to win."

Nancy frowned. "You look just like your sister. How could they think she was the pretty one instead of seeing that you were both lovely?"

"Oh, *Jill* wasn't the pretty one. Jill got to be the smart one, with expectations and standards she was supposed to live up to. *I* was the pretty one." Jack's smile was quick, lopsided, and wry. "If we both asked for Lego, she got scientists and dinosaurs, and I got a flower shop. If we both asked for shoes, she got sneakers, and I got ballet flats. They never asked us, naturally. My hair was easier to brush one day when we were toddlers—probably because she had jam in hers—and bam, the roles were set. We couldn't get away from them. Until one day we opened an old trunk and found a set of stairs inside."

Jack's voice had gone distant. Nancy held herself in perfect stillness, not speaking, barely daring to breathe. If she wanted to hear this story, she couldn't interrupt it. Something about the way Jack was glaring at the wall told her she was only going to get one chance.

"We went down the mysterious stairs that couldn't possibly be there, of course. Who *wouldn't* go down an impossible staircase in the bottom of a trunk? We were twelve. We were curious, and angry with our parents, and angry with each other." Jack tied her bow tie with quick, furious jerks. "We went down, and at the bottom there was a door, and on the door there was a sign. Two words. BE SURE. Sure of what? We were *twelve,* we weren't sure of *anything.* So we went through. We came out on this moor that seemed to go on forever, between the mountains and the angry sea. And that sky! I'd never seen so many stars before, or such a red, red moon. The door slammed shut behind us. We couldn't have gone back if we'd wanted to—and we didn't want to. *We were twelve.* We were going to have an adventure if it killed us."

"Did you?" asked Nancy. "Have an adventure, I mean?"

"Sure," said Jack bleakly. "It didn't even kill us. Not permanently, anyway. But it changed everything. I finally got to be the smart one. Dr. Bleak taught me everything he knew about the human body, the ways of recombining and reanimating tissue. He said I was the best pupil he'd ever had. That I had incredibly talented hands." She looked at her fingers like she was seeing them for the first time. "Jill went in a different direction. The world we went to, it was . . . feudal, almost, divided into villages and moors and protectorates, with a master or mistress holding sway over each of them. Our Master was a bloodsucker, centuries old, with a fondness for little girls—not like that! Not in any sort of inappropriate way. Even Dr. Bleak was a child to him, and the Master wasn't the sort of man who thought about children like that. But he did need blood to live. He made Jill a lot of promises. He told her she could be his daughter one day and rule alongside him. I guess that's why it was so important we be taken care of. When the villagers marched on the castle, he sent my sister to hide with me in the laboratory. Dr. Bleak said . . . he, uh, said it was too dangerous for us to stay, and he opened a doorway. Neither of us wanted to go, but I understood the necessity. I promised I would stay a scientist, no matter what else happened, and that one day, I'd find a way back to him. Jill—he had to sedate her before she would go through. We found ourselves back in that old trunk, the lid half closed and the stairway gone. I've been looking for the formula to unlock the way back for the both of us ever since."

"Oh," said Nancy, in a hushed voice.

Jack smiled that wry smile again. "Spending five years apprenticed to a mad scientist sort of changes your outlook on the world. I know Kade hates the fact that he had to go through puberty twice—he thinks it was unfair, and I guess for him, it was. Gender dysphoria is a form of torture. But I wish we'd gotten the same deal. We were twelve when we went into that trunk. We were seventeen when we came out. Maybe we would have been able to adapt to this stupid, colorful, narrow-minded world if we'd woken from a shared dream and been thrown straight into middle school. Instead, we staggered down the stairs and found our parents having dinner with our four-year-old brother, who'd been told for his entire life that we were dead. Not missing. That would have been *messy*. God forbid that we should ever make a *mess*."

"How long have you been here?" asked Nancy.

"Almost a year," said Jack. "Dearest Mommy and Daddy had us on the bus to boarding school within a month of our coming home. They couldn't stand to have us under the same roof as their precious boy, who didn't tell crazy stories about watching lightning snake down from the heavens and shock a beautiful corpse back into the land of the living." Her eyes went soft and dreamy. "I think the rules were different there. It was all about science, but the science was magical. It didn't care about whether something *could* be done. It was about whether it *should* be done, and the answer was always, always *yes*."

There was a knock at the door. Nancy and Jack both turned to see Kade stick his head inside.

"The crowd has mostly dissipated, but I have to ask: Jack, did you kill Sumi?"

"I'm not offended that you'd suspect me, but I'm offended that you think I'd kill for a pair of hands," said

Jack. She sniffed, squaring her shoulders. She looked suddenly imperious, and Nancy realized how much of Jack's superior attitude was just a put-on, something to keep the world a little more removed. "If *I* had killed Sumi, there would have been no body to find. I would have put every scrap of her to good use, and people would be wondering for years whether she'd finally managed to pry open the door that would take her back to Candyland. Alas, I didn't kill her."

"She called it Confection, not Candyland, but point taken." Kade stepped into the room. "Seraphina and Loriel have taken Jill someplace quiet while we wait for everyone to calm down. We're supposed to stay in our rooms and out of sight while Eleanor summons the city coroner."

Nancy stiffened. "What's going to happen to us now?" she asked. "They're not going to send us away, are they?" She couldn't go back. Her parents loved her, there was no question of that, but their love was the sort that filled her suitcase with colors and kept trying to set her up on dates with local boys. Their love wanted to *fix* her, and refused to see that she wasn't broken.

"Eleanor's been here for a long time," said Kade. He shut the door. "Sumi was her ward, so there are no parents to involve, and the local authorities know what's what. They'll do their best to make sure this doesn't shut us down."

"It would have been better had she not called at all," sniffed Jack. "An unreported death is just a disappearance in its Sunday clothes."

"See, it's things like that that explain why you don't have many friends," said Kade.

"But Sumi was among them," said Jack. She turned to look at Sumi's side of the room. "If she has no family, what are we supposed to do about her things?"

"There's storage space in the attic," said Kade.

"So we box them up," said Nancy firmly. "Where can we get some boxes?"

"The basement," said Jack.

"I'll go with you," said Kade. "Nancy, you stay here. If anyone asks, we'll be right back."

"All right," said Nancy, and held herself perfectly still as the others walked away. There was nothing left to do but wait. There was peace in stillness, a serenity that couldn't be found anywhere else in this hot, fast, often terrible world. Nancy closed her eyes and breathed down into her toes, letting her stillness become the only thing that mattered. Flashes of Sumi kept breaking her concentration, making it difficult to keep her knees from shaking or her fingers from twitching. She forced the images away and kept breathing, looking for serenity.

She still hadn't managed to find it when the others returned, the door banging open to Kade's declaration of "We are ready to box the world!"

Nancy opened her eyes and turned toward him, somehow mustering a smile. "All right," she said. "Let's get to work."

Sumi's things were as tangled and chaotic as Sumi had been. There was neither rhyme nor reason to the way they were piled around her bed and dresser. A pile of books on candy making was tied together with a pair of training bras. A bouquet of roses folded out of playing cards was shoved under the bed, next to a frilly blue dress that didn't look like something Sumi would ever have worn and a roast beef sandwich about a month past its "best by" date. Jack, who had put on gloves before they got to work, disposed of all the soiled or biologically questionable material without complaint: apparently, her squeamishness extended only as far as her bare skin. Kade sorted through Sumi's clothing, folding it neatly before boxing it up. Nancy was fairly sure it would all wind up back in the big group wardrobe. She was okay with that. Sumi wouldn't mind other people wearing her clothes. She probably wouldn't have minded while she was alive; she certainly wasn't going to object now that she was dead.

Nancy found herself tasked with handling the rest, the things that were neither trash nor fabric. She dug boxes of origami paper and embroidery floss from under the bed— Sumi had apparently always been good with her hands— and pushed them to one side, still digging. Her questing hands found a shoebox. She pulled it out and sat, removing the lid. Photos spilled onto the floor. Some showed Sumi as she'd been during their too-short acquaintance, mismatched clothing and tousled pigtails. Others showed a solemn, sad-eyed girl in a school uniform, sometimes holding a violin, other times empty-handed. It was plain, just from the still images, that this had been a girl who understood the virtue of being overlooked, of being a statue, but not because she had chosen stillness as Nancy had; it had been thrust upon her, until one day she'd discovered a door that could lead her to a world where she had a prayer of being happy.

Nancy realized that Sumi's granddaughter was never going to visit the candy corn farmer's grave, and it took everything she had not to weep for what had been irrevocably lost. Sumi might go to the Halls of the Dead, might even be happy there, but all the things she would have done among the living were gone now, rendered impossible when her heart stopped beating. Death was precious. That didn't change the fact that life was limited.

"Poor kid." Kade leaned over and took the picture from Nancy's motionless fingers, looking at it for a moment before he tucked it into his shirt. "Let's get this stuff out of here. You shouldn't have to look at it, not with her gone."

"Thank you," said Nancy, more earnestly than she would have believed before she'd seen that picture. Sumi was over, and it wasn't fair.

Working together, it took the three of them less than an hour to transfer all of Sumi's possessions to the attic, tucking the boxes away on unused shelves and in dusty corners, of which there seemed to be more than the usual number. When they were done, Jack removed her gloves and began meticulously wiping her fingers on a fresh handkerchief. Kade pulled the picture out of his shirt and tacked it up on a bulletin board, next to a picture of Sumi as Nancy had known her, all bright eyes and brighter smile, hands slightly blurred, as if she'd been photographed in motion.

"I'll stay with you tonight, if you don't mind," said Kade. "It doesn't seem safe for you to sleep in there alone."

"I won't stay with you tonight, whether you mind or not," said Jack. "That room gets too much sun, and Jill has a tendency to sleepwalk when I'm not with her."

"You shouldn't leave her alone," said Kade. "Watch yourself, okay? A lot of people are looking for someone to blame, and you're the best scapegoat in the school."

"I always wanted to be best at something," said Jack philosophically.

"Great," said Kade. "Now let's be best at getting to class before we get a lecture from Lundy on punctuality."

They filed out of the attic. Nancy looked back at Sumi's pictures on the bulletin board, so quiet, so still. Then she turned off the light and closed the door.

5 SURVIVORS, FOR A TIME

MORNING CLASSES HAD BEEN canceled; they resumed after lunch. Maybe it was rushing things, but there was nothing else to do with an entire school's worth of anxious, uneasy students: routine would keep them from wandering off and frightening themselves to death in the aftermath of Sumi's murder. Even so, it was a strained routine. Homework was forgotten, questions written on chalkboards went unanswered, and even the teachers clearly wanted to be elsewhere. Going back to normal after someone had died was never easy. When that someone had been brutally killed, all bets were off.

Dinner was worse. Nancy was sitting across from Jack and Jill when the girl with the brown braids walked up to the table and dumped her soup over Jack's head. "Oops," she said, flatly. "I slipped."

Jack sat rigidly unmoving, soup dripping down her fore-head and running down her nose. Jill gasped, leaping to her feet. "Loriel!" she shrieked, the sound of her voice bringing all other conversation in the dining hall grinding to a halt. "How *could* you?"

"It was an accident," said Loriel. "Just like your sister there 'accidentally' took apart Angela's guinea pig, and 'accidentally' murdered Sumi. She's going to get caught, you know. This would all go a lot faster if she'd confess."

"Loriel sneezed in that before she poured it on you," said the girl's companion to Jack, a look of fake concern on her face. "Just thought you'd want to know."

Jack began to tremble. Then, still dripping soup, she jerked away from the table and bolted for the door, leaving Jill to run after her. Half the students burst out laughing. The other half stared after her in mute satisfaction, clearly condoning anything that made Jack miserable. She had already been tried and found guilty by a jury of her peers. All that remained was for the law to catch up.

"You're horrible," said a voice. Nancy was only a little surprised to realize that it was hers. She pushed back her chair, leaving her own dinner of grapes and cottage cheese relatively untouched, and glared at the two. "You're horrible people. I'm *glad* we didn't go through the same door, because I would hate to have traveled to a world that didn't teach its tourists any manners." She turned and stalked away, head held high, following the trail of soup out of the dining room and down the hall to the basement stairs.

"You walk slow, but you move fast. How do you *do*

that?" said Kade, catching up with her at the top of the stairs. He followed her gaze down into the darkness. "That's where the Addams twins live. They were in your room for a while, until the kid who had the basement before them graduated."

"Had he been to the same world?"

"No, he visited a race of mole people. I think he realized he enjoyed sunshine and bathing, and sort of gave up on the idea of going back."

"Oh." Nancy took a tentative step down. "Is she going to be all right?"

"Jack doesn't like being messy. They have their own bathroom. She'll be all cleaned up and back in tip-top faintly morbid shape before group is over." Kade shook his head. "I just hope this is as bad as it gets. Jack can handle a little soup, and she worked for a mad scientist; for her, the wrath of the locals is all part of a day's work. But if people want to get violent, she'll fight back, and that'll just prove that they were in the right to accuse her."

"This is awful," said Nancy. "I let my parents send me here because Miss West said she understood what had happened to me and could help me learn how to live with it."

"And because you were hoping that if you understood it, you'd be able to do it again," said Kade. Nancy didn't say anything. He laughed ruefully. "Hey, it's okay. I understand. Most of us are here because we want to be able to open our doors at will, at least at first. Sometimes the desire goes away. Sometimes the door comes back. Sometimes we just have to learn to deal with being exiles in our home countries."

"What if we can't?" asked Nancy. "What happens to us then?"

Kade was silent for a long moment. Then he shrugged, and said, "I guess we open schools for people who still have what we want most in the world. Hope."

"Sumi said 'hope' was a bad word."

"Sumi wasn't wrong. Now come on. Let's get to group before we get in trouble."

They walked silently through the halls, and they saw no one moving in the rooms around them. The idea that sticking together was the only way to be safe seemed to have taken root with preternatural speed. Nancy found herself matching her steps to Kade's, hurrying to keep up with his longer stride. She didn't like hurrying. It was indecorous and would have resulted in a scolding back ho—back in the Underworld. Here, however, it was necessary, even encouraged, and there was no reason to feel guilty about it. She tried to hold to that thought as she and Kade stepped into the room where group was being held.

Everyone turned to look at them. Loriel actually sneered. "Couldn't get the little killer out of her basement?"

"That's quite enough, Miss Youngers," said Lundy sharply. "We have already agreed to stop speculating about who may have harmed Sumi."

She gets a name now, not a title and surname, thought Nancy. *That's not right. The dead deserve more dignity, not less. Dignity is all the dead possess.* Aloud, she said nothing, only made her way to an open chair and sat. She was gratified when Kade took the seat next to her. Loriel's glare intensified. Apparently Nancy wasn't the only one who found Kade beautiful, although she would have been willing to bet she was the only one who found his beauty more aesthetic than romantic.

"*You* agreed," said Loriel. "The rest of us are scared. Who would kill her like that? And mutilating the body afterward? That's just sick. We have a right to want to know what's going on, and how to keep ourselves safe!"

"I'm reasonably sure she bled out from her injuries, given the mess; corpses don't bleed as much," said Jack. Everyone in the room turned to see the twins, freshly scrubbed and wearing clean clothes, as they made their entrance. Jack looked more the old-fashioned professor than ever, wearing a tweed vest over a long-sleeved white shirt that buttoned at the wrists. Jill was wearing a cream-colored gown that Nancy would have considered sleepwear, not something to wear to group therapy. "Whoever killed her was no scientist."

"What do you mean?" asked one of the few boys, a tall Latino kid who was spinning a long piece of wood carved to resemble an ulna between his fingers. Nancy felt an odd kinship when she looked at him. Perhaps he'd been to someplace like her Underworld, filled with shadows, secrets, and safety. Perhaps he would understand if she went to him and spoke of stillness and respect for the dead.

But this was not the time. Jack met the question with a haughty sniff, and a too-calm, "I saw her body, like the rest of you. I know some of you have decided that I'm responsible for her death. I know further that those of you who believe my guilt will probably refuse to believe anything else. Draw on what you know of me. If I had decided to start killing my classmates, would I have left a body?"

The boy with the bone raised an eyebrow. "She makes a good point," he said.

"Making a good point doesn't mean she's not a killer," said Loriel, but the heat was gone; her accusations had been met with reality, and they didn't have anyplace else to go. She crossed her arms and slouched back in her chair. "I'm keeping an eye on her."

"Good," said Lundy. "We all need to be keeping our eyes on each other right now. We don't know who hurt Sumi. Eleanor is working with the authorities, and we should know more soon, but in the meantime, we need to be watching out for one another. No one goes anywhere alone—yes, Miss Youngers?"

Loriel lowered her hand as the attention of the group switched back to her. "What if one of us finds our door before the killer's caught?" she asked. "I can't take someone through with me just because we're not supposed to go anywhere alone, and I am *not* missing the passage back over this. I'm *not*."

"I think we can all agree that if someone happens to find their door while we're still staying together, the person whose door has been found will go, and the person who is left behind will find another buddy," said Lundy, with deliberate precision. Nancy realized with a start that Lundy didn't think any of them were going to find their doors. Not soon; maybe not ever. Lundy had given up on them. It was clear by her tone and by the way she chose her words. And maybe that made sense. Lundy's doors were closed, no matter where things went from here. Lundy needed to adapt to the idea that this was the world where she was going to die.

"Try for groups of three," said the boy with the bone. "If you can't manage that, try not to find your door."

Some of the students laughed. Others looked pained. Loriel was among the latter.

"Tell us about your door, Miss Youngers," urged Lundy.

"I almost didn't see it," said Loriel. Her voice turned distant. "It was so small. This perfect little door, carved into the lintel below the porch light. Like a door for moths. I just wanted to see what it was, that was all, so I got up really close, and I knocked with the tip of my pinkie finger. The world went all twisty and strange, and then I was standing in the hall on the other side of the door, looking back on this impossibly huge porch. I didn't go through. It pulled me. That was how bad the Webworld wanted me."

Loriel's story was grand and sprawling, a majestic, epic tale of spider princesses and tiny dynasties. Her eyes had always been keen, but after spending a year in service to the smallest, they had sharpened so much that she had to wear lenses made of carnival glass to keep the world from being so magnified that it was painful to behold. She had fought and she had triumphed, she had loved and she had lost, until finally the Queen of Dust had asked if she would become a princess of the land and stay forever.

"I said I wanted nothing more, but that I had to go home and tell my parents before I could accept," said Loriel, sniffling. The tears had started to fall somewhere around the death of her beloved Wasp Prince, and seemed set to continue for the foreseeable future. "She told me it would be hard to find the door again. That I would have to look harder than I had ever looked in my life. I said I could do it. That was almost two years ago. I've looked everywhere, but I haven't seen my door."

"Some doors open only once," said Lundy. There was a murmur of agreement from the room. Nancy frowned and sank deeper into her seat. It seemed cruel to dredge up everyone's pasts like this, pin them quivering to the floor, and then say things like that. Loriel surely knew by now that she probably wasn't going back through her tiny door to her even tinier world. She was smart enough to have figured it out for herself. What was the point in saying it?

If this was the school for those who wanted to come to peace with their voyages and remember them fondly, she would have hated to see the other campus.

"She said I could come back," said Loriel. "She promised me. Queens keep their promises. I just have to look more closely. Once I find the door, I'm gone."

"And your parents? Are they prepared for this inevitable disappearance?"

Loriel snorted. "I told them where I'd been—a year for

me, twelve days for them—and they said I'd clearly been through some trauma and couldn't be trusted. They sent me here so I'd stop being crazy. But there's nothing *wrong* with me. I went on a journey. That's all."

"A journey to a documented world, even," said Eleanor. She was standing in the doorway, new lines of exhaustion graven in the soft skin around her mouth and eyes. She looked like she had aged a decade in a day. "There have been five children pulled into the Webworld since I began seeking you all out. Two of them found their way back again after returning home. So you see, there *is* hope. For Loriel, and for all of us. Our doors are hidden, but by looking closely enough, we can find them."

"Eleanor." Lundy stood. "You're supposed to be resting."

"I've had rest enough to last a lifetime, and only a lifetime for the rest of what's to be done," said Eleanor. She moved away from the door. Several students rose to help her to an open chair. She smiled, patting at their cheeks. "Good children, all of you—yes, even you, Lundy. You're all children to me, and I your teacher, the only one who refuses to lie to you. So listen to me now, because it sounds like you're doing a fine job of confusing and upsetting yourselves.

"You will not all find your doors again. Some doors really do appear only once, the consequence of some strange convergence that we can't predict or re-create. They're drawn by need and by sympathy. Not the emotion—the resonance of one thing to another. There's a reason you were all pulled into worlds that suited you so well. Imagine, for a moment, if you'd fallen into the world described by your neighbor instead."

Nancy glanced at Jack and Jill, uneasily imagining what her life would have been like if she'd found their door instead of her own. The moors didn't seem to care about stillness, only obedience and blood. Neither of those things were strong suits of hers. All around her, other students exchanged equally uncomfortable glances, making their own connections and finding them just as unpleasant as she did.

"Sumi had Nonsense in her heart, and so a door opened that would take her to a world where she could wear it proudly, not hide it away. That was her real story. Finding a place where she could be free. That's your story, too, every one of you." Eleanor tipped her chin up. Her eyes were clear. "You found freedom, if only for a moment, and when you lost it, you came here, hoping it could be found again. I hope the same, for each of you. I want to make excuses to your parents when you disappear, to tell them that runaways will always run again if they have half the chance. I want to see the back of you more than I want almost anything in this world."

What she wanted most didn't need to be spoken, for they shared her hunger, her brutal, unforgiving desire: what she wanted most was a door, and the things that waited on its other side. But unlike the rest of them, she knew where her door was. It was simply closed to her for the time being, until she could find her way back to childhood.

The boy with the wooden bone put his hand up. "Eleanor?"

"Yes, Christopher?"

"Why did your door stay, while all ours disappeared?" He bit his lip before adding, "It doesn't seem fair for it to work like that. We should have been able to go back."

"Stable doors like Miss West's are less common than the temporary kind," said Lundy, back on familiar ground. "Most children who go through them don't come back, either on their first trip or after making a short return to their original world. So while we have records of several, the chances of finding a stable door that resonates with the story you need are slim."

"What about, like, Narnia?" asked Christopher. "Those kids went through all sorts of different doors, and they always wound up back with the big talking lion."

"That's because Narnia was a Christian allegory pretending to be a fantasy series, you asshole," said one of the other boys. "C. S. Lewis never went through any doors. He didn't know how it worked. He wanted to tell a story, and he'd probably heard about kids like us, and he made shit up. That's what all those authors did. They made shit up, and people made them famous. We tell the truth, and our parents throw us into this glorified loony bin."

"We don't use terms like that here," said Eleanor. There was steel in her tone. "This is not an asylum, and you are not mad—and so what if you were? This world is unforgiving and cruel to those it judges as even the slightest bit outside the norm. If anyone should be kind, understanding, accepting, loving to their fellow outcasts, it's you. All of you. You are the guardians of the secrets of the universe, beloved of worlds that most will never dream of, much less see . . . can't you see where you owe it to yourselves to be *kind*? To care for one another? No one outside this room will ever understand what you've been through the way the people around you right now understand. This is not your home. I know that better than most. But this is your way station and your sanctuary, and you will treat those around you with respect."

Both boys wilted under her glare. Christopher looked down. The other boy mumbled, "Sorry."

"It's all right. It's late, and we're all tired." Eleanor stood. "Get some sleep, all of you. I know it won't be easy. Nancy, can you—"

"I already said I'd room with her tonight," said Kade. A wave of relief washed over Nancy. She'd been afraid she would have to go to another room, and while she hadn't been there long, she was already attached to the familiarity of her own bed.

Eleanor looked at Kade thoughtfully. "Are you sure? I was going to suggest she room with someone on her hall, and that you lock your door tonight. This is a great imposition."

"No, it's fine. I volunteered." Kade flashed a quick smile. "I like Nancy, and she was Sumi's friend. I figure a little stability will do her good, and that makes any inconvenience to me completely beside the point. I want to help. This is my home." He looked slowly around the room. "My *forever* home. I turned eighteen last month, my parents don't want me, and the Prism wouldn't have me back even if I wanted to go. So it's important to me that we take care of this place, because it's been taking care of all of us since the day we got here."

"Go to bed, my darlings," said Eleanor. "This will all look better in the morning."

THE BODY LAY in the front yard, covered in a thin sheen of dew, face turned up toward the uncaring sky. The dead were capable of sight, as Nancy would have been quick to point out had she been asked, but this body saw nothing, for it had no eyes, only black and blood-rimmed holes where eyes had once been. Its hands were folded neatly on its chest, glasses clutched in cooling fingers. Loriel Youngers would never find her door (which had been waiting for her all this time, tucked into a corner of her bedroom at home, half an inch high and held in place by the most complicated magics the Queen of Dust, her adopted mother, could conceive; it would linger another six months before the spells were released and the Queen took to her chambers for a year of mourning). She would never have another grand adventure or save another world. Her part in the story was over.

She lay there, unmoving, as the sun rose and the stars winked out. A crow landed on the grass near her leg, watching her warily. When she still didn't move, it hopped on her knee, waiting for the trap to spring. When she *still* didn't move, it launched itself into the air and flew the few short feet to her head, where it promptly buried its beak in the bloody hole that had been her left eye.

Angela—she of the dissected guinea pig, whose enchanted sneakers had once allowed her to run on rainbows—was just stepping out onto the porch, rubbing the sleep from her eyes and intending to scold her roommate for sneaking out when they were supposed to stay together. Sometimes Loriel couldn't keep her eyes closed long enough to fall asleep, and then she had a tendency to roam the grounds, looking for her missing door. It wasn't unusual to find her dozing on the lawn. At first, Angela's mind refused to register Loriel's motionless body as anything unusual.

Then the crow pulled its bloody beak out of her eye socket and cawed at Angela, angrily protesting the interruption of its breakfast.

Angela's scream sent the crow flapping off into the morning sky. It didn't wake Loriel.

6 THE BODIES WE HAVE BURIED

ALL THE STUDENTS had been gathered in the dining hall, most dragged from their beds by either Angela's shrieks or the staff pounding on their doors. Nancy had been jerked awake by Kade shaking her shoulder, leaning so close that she could see the delicate filigree pattern of lines in his irises. She had jerked away, blushing and clutching the sheets around herself. Kade had only laughed, turning his back like a gentleman while she got up and put her clothes on.

Now, sitting at a table with a plate of scrambled eggs getting cold in front of her, Nancy found herself clinging to the memory of his laughter. She had the feeling that no one was going to be laughing here for quite some time. Maybe not ever again.

"Loriel Youngers was found dead this morning on the

front lawn," said Lundy, standing ramrod straight in front
of them, her hands folded in front of her. She looked like
a porcelain doll on the verge of shattering. "I was against
telling you anything more than that. I don't feel that such
morbid things are appropriate for the ears of young people.
But this is Miss West's school, and she felt your knowing
what had happened might make you take her request that
you stay together more seriously. Miss Youngers was found
without her eyes. They had been . . . removed. We thought
at first that it might have been predation by local wildlife,
but a closer study of the body showed that they had been
removed with a sharp object."

No one asked what kind of sharp object. Not even
Jack, although Nancy could see that she was practically
vibrating from keeping her questions contained. Jill, in con-
trast, seemed perfectly serene, and was one of the few students who was actually eating. Spending a few years in a
horror movie must have done a great deal to harden her
sensibilities.

"Unlike Sumi, Loriel's parents were still involved with
her care, and we have not yet contacted the authorities."
There was a catch in Lundy's voice. "Eleanor is in her chambers, deciding what to do. Please, finish your breakfasts
and then return to your rooms. Do not go anywhere alone,
not even the restrooms. The school is not safe." She turned,
not waiting for them to respond to her, and walked quickly
to the exit.

When she was gone, Jack finally frowned and let one of
her questions out. "Eleanor sat there last night and said she

was looking forward to lying to our parents about what happened to us," she said. "Why can't she just make Loriel disappear, and tell that lie?"

"Not everyone is as comfortable as you are with the idea of getting rid of bodies," said Angela through her tears. She had been crying since finding Loriel's body. It didn't look like she was ever intending to stop.

"It's not a bad question," said Christopher. He touched his bone nervously as he spoke. For the first time, Nancy wondered if it might be real, instead of wood as she had first assumed. "Miss West already has a system in place for making it look like we ran away when we really went home. Why shouldn't she lie to Loriel's family? They lost her either way. At least a lie means we can all stay here, instead of going back."

"Going back" had two distinct meanings at the school, depending on how it was said. It was the best thing in the world. It was also the worst thing that could happen to anybody. It was returning to a place that understood you so well that it had reached across realities to find you, claiming you as its own and only; it was being sent to a family that wanted to love you, wanted to keep you safe and sound, but didn't know you well enough to do anything but hurt you. The duality of the phrase was like the duality of the doors: they changed lives, and they destroyed them, all with the same, simple invitation. *Come through, and see.*

"I don't want to stay in a place where we just make bodies go away," said Angela. "That isn't why I came here."

"Get off your high horse," snapped Jack. "Bodies are a consequence of life. Or do you truly mean for us to believe that when you were running along rainbows, you never saw anyone fall? Someone plummets out of the sky, they're not going to get up and walk away from it. They're going to die. And unless they fell into a place like the Moors, they're going to stay dead. Someone disposed of those bodies. One slip, and they'd have been disposing of yours."

Angela stared at Jack, eyes wide and horrified. "I never thought about it," she said. "I saw . . . I saw people fall. The rainbows were slippery. Even with the right shoes, you could fall through if you slowed down too much."

"Someone disposed of those bodies," said Jack. "Ashes to ashes, right? If we call Loriel's parents, if we tell them what happened, that's it, we're done. Anyone who's under eighteen gets taken home by their loving parents. Half of you will be on antipsychotic drugs you don't need before the end of the year, but hey, at least you'll have someone to remind you to eat while you're busy contemplating the walls. The rest of us will be out on the streets. No high school degrees, no way of coping with this world, which doesn't want us back."

"At least you have prospects," said Christopher, giving his bone another spin. "How many colleges you been accepted to?"

"Every one that I've applied to, but they're all assuming I'll graduate before I come knocking," said Jack. "And of course, I've Jill to consider. I can't go running out into the world without making provisions for my sister."

"I can take care of myself," said Jill.

"You won't have to," said Eleanor. She walked wearily into the room, looked toward Jack and Kade, and said, "Make her go away, darlings. Put her someplace where I'll never find her, not if I look for a thousand years. We'll have a memorial service. We'll honor her as best we can. But I can't endanger us all because of one lost life. I almost wish I could. I would feel less like a monster, and more like the child who danced with foxes under the slow October moon. I simply cannot bring myself to do it."

"Of course," said Jack, and started to stand.

Angela was on her feet first. "She *killed* her, and now you're going to let her have the body?" she shrilled, pointing at Jack. Her face was a mask of outrage. "She's a murderess! Loriel knew it, I know it, and I can't believe that *you* don't know it!"

"Points for knowing the feminine form of 'murderer,' although I'm a little insulted that you feel the need to put a lacy bow on the crime before you can believe I committed it," said Jack. "What would I do with a pair of eyes, Angela? I don't care about the visual sciences. I'm sure there were some fascinating adaptations to her cones and rods, but I don't have the facilities or equipment here to study them. If I were going to kill her for her eyes, I would have done it in ten years, after I was nicely established as the head of research and development for a biotech firm big enough to make murder charges just go away. Killing her now benefits me not at all."

"Can we stop pointing fingers at each other and *deal*

with this? Please?" Kade stood. "We already have one body
on our hands. I don't want any more."

"I can help," said Nancy. The others turned toward her.
She reddened slightly, but pushed on, saying, "I can make
sure nothing is done that's not respectful toward the
dead. The flesh they leave behind when they depart doesn't
bother me."

"You're a creepy girl," said Christopher approvingly. He
stood, tucking his bone into his pocket. "I'll help as well.
The Skeleton Girl would never forgive me if I didn't."

"I won't," said Jill. "It would ruin my dress."

"Thank you, all of you," said Eleanor. "Classes have been
canceled for the rest of the morning. We'll see you after
lunch, once you've had time to put yourselves together
again."

"Bad choice of words," said Jack—but she looked
thoughtful, almost pensive, as she turned her face away and
led Kade and Nancy out of the room. Christopher brought
up the rear, his bone sticking out of his back pocket like
an upthrust middle finger. The door swung closed behind
him.

Together, they walked out to the porch. Loriel was still
on the lawn, covered by a sheet, and for a moment, all
Nancy could think was that if this didn't stop soon, they
were going to run out of bedclothes. Nancy, Christopher,
and Jack kept walking. Kade stopped.

"I'm sorry," he said. "I can't. I just . . . I *can't*. This was
never my job." Because he'd been a princess in Prism, before they'd learned that he was really a prince; because

unlike the rest of them, he had never been responsible for tending to the dead. He'd killed people, sure. That was what had earned him the title of Goblin Prince. But his part in their deaths had ended on the blade of his sword.

"It's all right," said Nancy gently, looking back over her shoulder at him. "The dead are much more understanding than the living. Let us take care of her. You keep watch."

"I can do that," said Kade, relieved.

Nancy, Jack, and Christopher made their way to the body. They came from very different traditions. For Nancy, the entire experience of death was revered. For Christopher, the flesh was temporary, but the bones were eternal and deserved to be treated as such. For Jack, death was an inconvenience to be conquered, and a corpse was a Pandora's box of beautiful possibilities. But all of them shared a love for those who had passed, and as they lifted Loriel from the ground, they did so with gentle, compassionate hands.

"If we take her to the basement, I can mix up something to strip the flesh from her bones," said Jack. "The skeleton will still appear fresh to any forensics tests, but it's a start."

"Once she's a skeleton, I might be able to find out what happened to her," said Christopher, sounding almost shy.

There was a pause. Finally, dubiously, Jack said, "I'm sorry, but it sounded like you just confessed to being able to talk to bones. Why have we never heard this before?"

"Because I was there when you said you could raise the dead. I saw how everybody reacted, and I enjoy having a social life at this school," said Christopher. "It's not like I can go hang out at the pizza parlor in town if the other kids stop talking to me. And don't say you and your sister would have talked to me. The two of you don't talk to *anybody*."

"He's got you there," called Kade from the porch.

Nancy frowned. "They talked to me."

"Because Sumi made them, and because you went to a world full of ghosts," said Christopher. "I guess that was close enough to living in a horror movie that they were cool with you. And they talked to Sumi because she didn't give them a *choice*. Sumi was like a small tornado. When she sucked you up, you just tightened your grip and went along for the ride."

"We keep to ourselves for good reason," said Jack stiffly, adjusting her grasp on Loriel's shoulders. "Most of you got unicorns and misty meadows. We got the Moors, and if there was a unicorn out there, it probably ate human flesh. We learned quickly that sharing our experiences with others just drove them away, and most of the social connections at this place are based on those shared experiences. On the doors, and on what happened when we went through them."

"I went to a country of happy, dancing skeletons who said that one day I'd come back to them and marry their Skeleton Girl," said Christopher. "So pretty sunshiny, but sort of sunshine by way of Día de los Muertos."

"Maybe we should have talked to you a long time ago," said Jack. "Let's get Loriel to the basement."

They carried her around the side of the manor, walking until they found the ground-level doors that had once been used by tradesmen delivering coal or food to the house above. Their hands were full, and so Nancy twisted to look over her shoulder as she called, "Kade? We need you."

"This I can do," said Kade. He jogged past them and opened the cellar doors, releasing a rush of cool, sepulchral air. He held the doors until the others were through, and then he followed them, closing the doors with a final-sounding *clank* that left them in near darkness. Nancy had dwelt in the Halls of the Dead, where the lights were never turned above twilight, for fear of hurting sensitive eyes. Christopher had learnt to navigate a world of skeletons, none of whom *had* eyes anymore, and many of whom had long since forgotten about the squishy living and their need for constant illumination. Jack could see by the light of a single storm. Only Kade stumbled, managing not to fall as the group made their way to the base of the stairs.

"Can you hold her up without me for a second?" asked Jack. "I should turn the lights on before one of you buffoons trips and damages something valuable."

"See, that's the other reason no one talks to you," said Christopher. "You're sort of mean, like, all the time. Even when you don't have any real reason to be. You could just say 'please.'"

"*Please* can you hold her up without me for a second, so that we don't knock over the jug of acid I was planning to use to dissolve her flesh," said Jack. "I enjoy having non-skeletal feet. Perhaps you do as well."

"For now," said Christopher. He shifted his grip around Loriel's torso, getting his arms locked. "All right, I think I have her."

"Excellent. I'll be right back." The body seemed to grow heavier in Nancy's and Christopher's arms as Jack let go. They heard her moving away, steps light on the concrete floor of the basement. Then, calmly, she said, "You may want to close your eyes."

They tensed, expecting a blazing surgical light. Instead, when she flipped the switch, a soft orange glow bathed the room, revealing metal racks filled with jars and lab equipment, dressers bulging with wispy lace and ribbons, and a stainless-steel autopsy table. There was only one bed.

Nancy made a small sound of dismay as she realized what this meant. "You sleep on the autopsy table?" she asked.

Jack touched the smooth metal with one hand. "Not much call for pillows or blankets in the lab," she said. "Jill got the canopy beds and the cushions. I learned how to sleep on stone floors. Turns out that sort of thing is hard to unlearn. Sleeping in a real bed is like trying to sleep in a cloud. I'm afraid I'll sink right through and fall to my death." She sighed, taking her hand off the autopsy table. "Put her here. I want to look at her before we dissolve her."

"Is this a creepy perv thing?" asked Christopher, as he and Nancy maneuvered the body through the lab. "I'm not sure I can stay to help if it's a creepy perv thing."

"I don't like corpses in that way unless they've been re-animated," said Jack. "Corpses are incapable of offering informed consent, and are hence no better than vibrators."

"I wish that didn't make so much sense," said Christopher. Together, he and Nancy boosted Loriel up onto the autopsy table. He let go and stepped away. Nancy remained, taking a moment to straighten the body's limbs and smooth out its hair. There was nothing she could do for the pits that had been Loriel's eyes—she couldn't even close them. In the end, she simply folded Loriel's hands over her chest and backed away.

Jack moved into the position Nancy had vacated. Unlike the other girl, she didn't shy away from the damage to Loriel's face. She leaned in close, studying the striations in the flesh, the way it had been torn and opened. Pulling on a pair of rubber gloves, she reached out and carefully rolled Loriel's head to the side, probing her skull with quick, careful motions. Nancy and Christopher watched closely, but nothing Jack was doing was disrespectful: if anything, she was showing more respect to Loriel now that she was dead than she ever had when the other girl was among the living.

Jack grimaced. "Her skull's been cracked," she said. "Someone hit her from behind hard enough to knock her down and disorient her. I can't say for sure whether it knocked her out. Knocking someone out is harder than most people guess. It was a blitz attack; she didn't have a chance to defend herself or scream for help before she was down. But it wouldn't have killed her right away. And there's quite a lot of blood in her sockets."

"Jack . . ." Kade's voice was low and horrified. "Please tell me you're not saying what I think you're saying."

"Hmm?" Jack looked up. "I'm not *psychic*, Kade, I don't even believe that psychics *exist*. There is no possible way I could read your mind and know what you think I'm saying. I'm simply talking about the manner in which Loriel's eyes were extracted."

"You mean removed?" asked Christopher.

"No, I mean extracted," said Jack. "I'd need to open her skull to be sure, and I don't have a proper bone saw, which makes that a difficult task, but it appears that her eyes were fully extracted, all the way along the optic nerve. Whoever assaulted her didn't just pluck them out like grapes. They used some sort of blade to separate the eye from the muscles holding it in place, and once that was done, they—"

"Do you know who did it?" asked Kade.

"No."

"Then please, stop telling us how it was done. I can't take it anymore."

Jack looked at him solemnly, and said, "I haven't gotten to the important part yet."

"Then please, get there, before the rest of us throw up on the floor."

"Based on the damage to the skull and the amount of bleeding, she was alive when her eyes were taken," said Jack. Silence greeted her proclamation. Even Nancy put a hand over her mouth. "Whoever did this subdued her, removed her eyes, and let the shock kill her. I'm not even sure her death was the goal. Just getting her eyes."

"Why?" asked Christopher.

Jack hesitated before shaking her head and saying, "I don't know. Come on. Let's prepare her for burial."

Kade retreated back to the far side of the basement and

stayed there as the others got to work. Nancy undressed Loriel, folding each piece of clothing with care before setting it aside. She somehow doubted that these clothes were going to make it into the general supply. They would probably need to be destroyed along with Loriel's body, just for the sake of safety.

While Nancy worked, Jack and Christopher pulled an old claw-footed bathtub out of a corner of the basement and into the center of the room. Jack uncorked several large glass jugs and poured their greenish, fizzing contents into the tub. Kade watched this with dismay.

"Why does Eleanor let you have that much acid?" he asked. "Why would you *want* that much acid? You don't need that much acid."

"Except that it appears I do, since I have just enough to dissolve a human body, and we have a human body in need of dissolving," said Jack. "Everything happens for a reason. And Eleanor didn't 'let' me have this much acid. I sort of collected it on my own. For a rainy day."

"What were you expecting it to rain?" asked Christopher. "Bears?"

"There was always a chance we'd get lucky," said Jack. She pulled several plastic aprons off a shelf and held them out to the others. "You're going to want to put one of these on, and a pair of the gloves that go with them. Acid is not a fun exfoliator unless you come from Christopher's world."

Wordlessly, Nancy and Christopher donned their plastic aprons, rubber gloves, and goggles. Jack did the same, and together they lowered Loriel into the fizzing green liquid.

Kade turned his face away. The smell was surprisingly pleasant, not meaty at all: it smelled like cleaning fluid, faintly citrus, with a minty undertone. The bubbles increased as Loriel disappeared beneath the surface, until the liquid was completely opaque, obscuring her from view. Jack turned away.

"It'll take about an hour to reduce her to a skeletal state," she said. "I'll neutralize the acid and drain it off when she's done. Christopher, do you think you can handle her from there?"

"She'll dance for me." Christopher touched the bone in his pocket. Nancy realized there were small indentations in the surface. Not holes, not quite, and yet it still managed to suggest a flute. The tunes he played on that instrument wouldn't be audible to the living. That didn't mean they wouldn't be real. "All skeletons dance for me. It's my honor to play for them."

"All right, clearly the two of you"—Jack gestured to Nancy as she stripped off her gloves—"were meant to be together. If you can't find your doors, you should get married and breed the next generation of creepy world-traveling children."

Christopher's cheeks turned red. Nancy's didn't. It was a pleasant change.

"Maybe we should figure out why people are dying before we start trying to set up a breeding program," said Kade mildly. "Besides, I met Nancy first. I get asking-out dibs."

"Sometimes I suspect you learned all your hallmarks of

masculinity from a Neanderthal," said Jack. She removed her apron, hanging it on a nearby hook. "Everyone please take off the gear you borrowed. That stuff is expensive, and I only get to place three orders a year."

"Do I get a say in this?" asked Nancy, shooting an amused look over at Kade. She didn't mind flirting. Flirting was safe, flirting was fun; flirting was a way of interacting with her peers without anyone realizing that there was anything strange about her. She could have flirted forever. It was just the things that came after flirting that she had no interest in.

"Maybe later," said Jack. "Right now, we need to get out of here. The acid will do some off-gassing as it breaks down her tissues, and I don't want to fill my lungs with Loriel. Besides, I shouldn't leave Jill alone for too long." She sounded uneasy.

"I'm sure no one will hurt your sister," said Nancy. "She can take care of herself."

"That's what I'm worried about," said Jack. "When you spend years with a vampire, all those lessons about 'don't bite the other children' sort of go out the window. If they corner her because they've decided I'm guilty, she's liable to hurt someone just so she can get away. I'd rather not get expelled right after I've disposed of a body. Seems like a waste of good acid."

"All right," said Nancy, pulling her apron off over her head. "Let's go."

Since they were no longer trying to spare their fellow students the sight of Loriel's body, the foursome walked up the interior stairs, emerging into the deserted hallway. Kade looked in both directions before turning to Jack and asking, "Where would she go?"

"How would I know?" asked Jack. She sighed when the others stared at her. "I'm her *twin*. I'm not her keeper. I'm not even her friend. We mostly stick together out of self-defense. The other girls think she's weird, and they think I'm weirder. At least when we present a united front, they're less likely to do things to us."

"Things?" asked Nancy blankly.

Jack fixed her with a look that was equal parts pitying and envious. "You didn't get a hazing phase. That's the real reason Eleanor put you in with Sumi. Once Sumi liked you—or at least tolerated you—no one else was going to cross the line, because everyone knew better than to mess with Sumi. She was vicious. Nonsense girls always are. Jill and I . . ."

"I remember when you got here," said Christopher. "I thought your sister was hot, you know? So I offered to show her around the school, figured maybe I could get in good before one of the other guys showed up and started talking about his magic sword and how he'd saved the universe or whatever. I'm a dude with a flute no one can hear. I have to be persistent."

"She laughed at you, didn't she?" Most people would have been surprised by the gentleness of Jack's tone. She wasn't the sort of person who seemed inclined to gentleness.

Christopher nodded. "She said I was a cute little boy,

but that she couldn't lower herself to be seen with me. Like, that was her opening statement. Not 'thanks, no thanks,' not 'my name's Jill.' Just straight to 'you're a cute little boy.' I stopped trying after that."

"She was trying to save you, in her way," said Jack. "Her Master was the jealous sort. She used to try to make friends with the kids from the village below his castle. Jill liked having a lot of friends around. Believe it or not, she used to be the gregarious one, even if it was a nerdy sort of friendly. She'd run you to ground to tell you about the latest episode of *Doctor Who*. This was early on, before she'd embraced the lacy dresses and the iron-rich diet. Back then, she thought we were just having an adventure. She was the one who thought we were going to go home someday and wanted to learn as much as she could."

"And you?" asked Kade.

"I gave up on wanting to go home the second Dr. Bleak put a bone saw in my hand and told me he would teach me anything I wanted to know," said Jack. "For a while, Jill was opening doors and looking for a road home, and I was the one who never wanted to leave."

"What happened to the kids from the village?" asked Christopher. "The ones she tried to make friends with?"

Jack's expression went blank. It wasn't coldness, exactly, more a means of *distancing* herself from what she was about to say. "We lived in the grace and at the sufferance of a vampire lord. What do you *think* happened to the kids from the village? Her Master didn't want her talking to anyone he couldn't control. I think he only spared me because

Dr. Bleak begged, and because he pointed out the wisdom in keeping a self-replenishing source of blood transfusions for Jill. We're twins. If anything happened to her, I could be used for spare parts."

Nancy's mouth dropped open. "That's *horrible*," she squeaked.

"That was the Moors." Jack shook her head. "It was cruel and cold and brutal and beautiful, and I would give anything to go back there. Maybe it broke me in some deep, intrinsic way that I am incapable of seeing, just like Jill can't understand that she's not a normal girl anymore. I don't care. It was my home, and it finally let me be myself, and I hate it here."

"We pretty much all hate it here," said Kade. "Even me. That's why we're at this school. Now think. Your sister isn't in the basement, so where would she go?"

"She might still be in the dining hall, since it's harder to pick on her when there's supervision around," said Jack. "Or she could have gone out to sit in the trees and pretend that she's back at home. We spent a lot of time outside there, for one reason or another."

"We saw her there yesterday," said Kade. "Nancy and I will go check the trees; you and Christopher check the dining hall. We'll meet back at the attic no matter what we find."

"Why the attic?" asked Christopher.

But Jack was nodding. "Good call. We can go through your books while Loriel finishes stewing. Maybe there's something in there about why someone would be harvesting parts from world-walkers. It's a long shot. At this point, I'll take it. Come on, bone boy." She turned and strode down the hall, every inch the confident mad scientist's protégée once again. Any vulnerability she had shown was gone, tamped down and covered over by the mask she wore.

"Thanks for sticking me with the scary girl," said Christopher to Kade, and ran after her, pulling the bone flute from his pocket.

"You're welcome," Kade called after him. He offered his arm to Nancy, grinning. "C'mon. Let's go see if we can't find ourselves an Addams." His drawl grew thicker, dripping from his words like sweet and tempting honey.

Nancy set her hand in the crook of his elbow, feeling the traitorous red creeping back into her cheeks. This was always the difficult part, back when she'd been at her old school: explaining that "asexual" and "aromantic" were different things. She *liked* holding hands and trading kisses. She'd had several boyfriends in elementary school, just like most of the other girls, and she had always found those practice relationships completely satisfying. It wasn't until puberty had come along and changed the rules that she'd started pulling away in confusion and disinterest. Kade was possibly the most beautiful boy she'd ever seen. She wanted to spend hours sitting with him and talking about pointless things. She wanted to feel his hand against her skin, to know that his presence was absolute and focused entirely on her. The trouble was, it never seemed to end there, and that was as far as she was willing to go.

Kade must have read her discomfort, because he flashed

her a smile and said, "I promise I'm a gentleman. You're as safe with me as you are with anyone who's not the murderer."

"And see, I was just trying to decide whether I thought you might be the killer," said Nancy. "I'm really relieved to hear that you're not. I'm not either, just for the record."

"That's good to know," said Kade.

They walked together through the deserted manor. Whispers sometimes drifted from the rooms they passed, indicating the presence of their fellow students. They didn't stop. Everyone had their own concerns, and Nancy had an uneasy feeling that by helping Jack destroy Loriel's body, she had just placed herself firmly in the "enemy" camp for anyone who had been a friend of Loriel's when she was alive. Nancy had never made so many enemies before, or so quickly. She didn't like it. She just didn't see a way to undo it.

There was no one outside. The lawn was empty as she and Kade walked toward the trees; even the crows had flown away, off to look for some richer pickings. Everything was silent, eerily so.

Jill wasn't in the trees. That was almost a disappointment: Nancy had been fully expecting to step into the sheltered grove and see the other girl sitting on a root, posed like something out of a gothic novel, with her parasol blocking out any stray sunbeams that had dared to come too close. Instead, the sun shone down undisturbed, and Nancy and Kade were alone.

"Well, that's one down," said Nancy, suddenly nervous.

What if Kade wanted to kiss her? What if Kade didn't want to kiss her? There was no good answer, and so she did what she always did when she was confused or frightened: she froze, becoming a girl-shaped statue.

"Whoa," said Kade. He sounded genuinely impressed. "That's some trick. Do you actually turn into stone, or does it only seem like you do?" He prodded her gently in the arm with one finger. "Nope, still flesh. You're holding really, really still, but you're not inanimate. How are you doing that? Are you even breathing? I can't do that."

"The Lady of Shadows required that everyone who served her be able to hold properly still," said Nancy, releasing her pose. Her cheeks reddened again. This was all going so *wrong*. "I'm sorry. I tend to freeze up when I get nervous."

"Don't worry, you're safe with me," said Kade. "Whoever the killer is, they're only striking when people are alone. We'll stick together, and we'll be fine."

But you're what I'm nervous about, thought Nancy. She forced a wan smile. "If you really think so," she said. "Jill isn't here. We should get back to the attic before Jack and Christopher start to worry about us."

They walked side by side back the way that they had come, Nancy's fingers resting on Kade's arm and her eyes scanning the grassy expanse of the lawn, looking for some clue as to what had happened. There had to be *something* that would bring all this together, that would force it to make sense. They couldn't just be at the mercy of an unseen killer, who slaughtered them for no apparent reason.

"Hands," she murmured.

"What's that?" asked Kade.

"I was just thinking about Sumi's hands," she said. "She was really good with her hands, you know? Like they were the most important thing about her. Maybe someone is trying to take away the things we treasure the most. I don't know why, though, or how they'd know."

"It makes sense," said Kade. They had reached the porch steps. As they started up, he said, "Most of the students lost the things that were most precious to them when their doors closed. Maybe someone's so heartbroken that they're trying to make sure nobody gets to be happy. If they have to be miserable, so does everyone else."

"But you're not miserable when you're dead," said Nancy.

"I sure do hope not," said Kade, and reached for the doorknob.

The door opened before he touched it.

7 COCOA

LUNDY STOOD IN the doorway, eyeing the pair suspiciously. "Where were you?"

"Morning to you, too, ma'am," said Kade. "We got Loriel sorted, just like Miss Eleanor asked us to, and then we went to find Jill. Jack and Christopher are looking inside; we went to look outside. Since she's not out here, do you mind if we come back in?"

"She shouldn't be alone," said Lundy, stepping to the side and holding the door wider to let them pass. "Why didn't you take her with you?"

"Getting blood out of her dress would have been really hard," said Nancy, without thinking about it. Lundy turned a startled, offended look on her, and she winced. "Um, sorry. It's true, though. You can't get blood out of taffeta, no matter how much you scrub."

"What fascinating life lessons you have to share," said Lundy. "Both of you need to get back inside. It's not safe out here." Her eyes stayed on Nancy, cold and judgmental.

Nancy shivered, trying not to let her unhappiness show. Her hand still bore down involuntarily on Kade's arm, tightening. "All right," she said. "We'll see you at lunch."

They walked past Lundy, past the gleaming chandelier with its dusting of frozen tears, and up the stairway to the attic. Only when they were standing outside the door did Nancy allow her fingers to unclench and the shaking that had been threatening to overwhelm her to take over. She sank to the floor, pressing her back to the wall and pulling her knees up against her chest.

Be still, she thought. *Be still, be still, be still.* But the shaking continued as her traitorous body betrayed her, trembling like a leaf in a hard wind.

"Nancy?" Kade sounded alarmed. He knelt next to her, putting his hand on her shoulder. "Nancy, what's wrong? Are you all right?"

"She thinks I did it." Her voice came out thin and reedy, but audible. She drew in a deep breath, forced her head away from her knees, and looked at Kade as she said, "Lundy thinks I did it. She thinks I'm the one who killed Sumi and Loriel. I come from a world full of ghosts. I'm closer to Jack and Jill than I am to anyone else here, and they've been here forever without killing anybody. But I show up, and people start dropping dead. Suspecting the new girl only makes sense. When the new girl doesn't mind helping with the bodies, it becomes almost too easy. She thinks I did it, because anything else would be complicated and hard."

"Lundy thinks in stories," said Kade, rubbing Nancy's back soothingly. "She spent too long in the Goblin Market before she made her bargain. She has stories in her blood. You're right about being the most logical suspect—new girl, no strong ties, came from an Underworld. You're probably right about Lundy suspecting you. But you're wrong if you think that Eleanor will let her hurt you. Eleanor knows you didn't do it, just like I do. Now come on. I have a hot plate and a teapot in the attic. I can make you something hot to drink, soothe your nerves."

"Actually, I already made cocoa," said Jack, opening the door and poking her head out. "Did you find my sister?"

"No, didn't you?" Kade looked over his shoulder and frowned. "I figured if we didn't find her, you would. Did you check the dining hall?"

"Yes, *and* the library, *and* the classroom we're supposed to be in this time of day, just in case she'd been so absorbed in thinking about her hair that she hadn't paid attention to what we were told to do," said Jack. Her frustration seemed only skin-deep, a cover for her all-too-real concern. "She wasn't in any of the places we looked. I was hoping you'd find her."

"Sorry." Kade stood, offering Nancy his hand. "We looked, we didn't find, we got a scolding from Lundy, and Nancy—"

"Had a little cry when she realized Lundy suspected her," finished Nancy, taking Kade's hand and pulling herself to her feet. "I'm better now. As long as Eleanor doesn't suspect me, I probably won't be expelled. Let's just stick together so that none of us gets hurt, and we'll ride this thing out as a group."

"Huh," said Jack, looking wistful. "I haven't been part of a group since we left our old school. Now come on. Like I said, I made hot chocolate, and Christopher will drink it all if we leave him alone too long."

"I heard that!" called Christopher. Jack snorted and withdrew into the attic.

Kade shot Nancy a worried look, which she answered with a smile and a reassuring squeeze of his hand before she let go and stepped into the attic ahead of him. As promised, the air smelled like hot chocolate. Christopher was sitting on one of the heaps of books, a mustache of whipped cream on his lip and a mug cupped in his hands. Jack was at the hot plate, fixing three more mugs. Kade raised an eyebrow.

"Where did you find the whipped cream?" he asked.

"You had milk, I had science," said Jack. "It's amazing how much of culinary achievement can be summarized by that sentence. Cheese making, for example. The perfect intersection of milk, science, and foolish disregard for the laws of nature."

"How did the laws of nature come into this?" asked Nancy, walking over to claim one of the mugs. The smell was alluring. She took a sip, and her eyes widened. "This tastes like . . ."

"Pomegranate, I know," said Jack. "Yours was made with

pomegranate molasses. Christopher's has a pinch of cinnamon, and Kade's contains clotted cream fudge, which I stole from Miss Eleanor's private supply. She'll never notice. She has the stuff shipped over from England by the pound, and her next delivery is due in three days."

"What's in yours?" asked Nancy.

Jack smiled, holding her mug up in a silent toast. "Three drops of warm saline solution and a pinch of wolfsbane. Not enough to be dangerous to me—I'm human, despite what Angela might say to the contrary—but enough to make it taste like tears, and like the way the wind smells when it sweeps along the moor at midnight. If I knew the taste of the sound of screaming, I'd add that as well, and never drink anything again, as long as I chanced to live."

Christopher swallowed a mouthful of cocoa, shook his head, and said, "You know, sometimes I almost forget how *creepy* you are, and then you go and say something like that."

"It's best if you remember my nature at all times," said Jack, and offered Kade his mug.

"Thank you," he said, taking it from her and wrapping his long fingers around it.

"Say nothing of it," said Jack. Somehow, coming from her, it wasn't politeness: it was a plea. *Let this momentary kindness be forgotten,* it said. *Don't let it linger, lest it be seen as weakness.* Outwardly, all she did was twitch one corner of her mouth in a transitory smile. Then she turned, hands cupping her own mug, and moved to find a seat on the piles of books.

"Isn't this cozy?" Kade returned to what seemed to be his customary perch, leaving Nancy standing awkward and alone next to the hot plate. She looked around before heading for one of the few actual pieces of furniture, an old-fashioned, velvet-covered chair that was being encroached upon by the books, but hadn't been swallowed yet. She sank down into its embrace, tucking her feet underneath her, hands still cupped around her mug.

"I like it," said Christopher, after it became apparent that no one else was going to say anything. He shrugged before he added, "The guys—uh, the other guys, I mean, not you, Kade—put up with me because there're so few of us here, but they all went to sparkly worlds. They all sort of think where I went was weird, so I can't talk to them about it much. They start insulting the Skeleton Girl and then I have to punch them in their stupid mouths until they stop. Not the best way to make friends."

"No, I suppose not," said Jack. She looked down at her cocoa. "I had similar issues when I attempted to make friends with my fellow students. I gave up trying before Jill did. All they ever wanted to do was talk about how strange the Moors must have been, and how inferior to their own cotton-candy wonderlands. Honestly, I don't blame them for thinking I could be a killer. I blame them for thinking I would have waited this long."

"And bonding just got creepy again," said Christopher cheerfully, before taking a gulp of his hot chocolate. "Luckily for you, I'll forgive anything for cocoa this good."

"Like I said, cooking is a form of science, and I am a scientist," said Jack.

"We do need to figure out what's going on," said Kade. "I don't know about the rest of you, but I'm not so well-equipped to go back to my old life. My parents still think they're somehow magically going to get back the little girl they lost. They haven't let me come home for five years. No, maybe that's unfair—or too fair. They won't let *me* come home. If I want to put on a skirt and tell them to call me 'Katie,' they'll welcome me with open arms. Pretty sure that if the school closes down, I'm homeless."

"My folks would let me come back," said Christopher. "They think this is all some complicated breakdown triggered by the things that happened after I 'ran away.' Mom genuinely believes the Skeleton Girl is some girl I fell for who died of anorexia. Like, she asks me on the regular whether I can remember her 'real name' yet, so they can track down her parents and tell them what happened to her. It's really sad, because they care so damn much, and they're so completely wrong about everything, you know? The Skeleton Girl is real, and she isn't dead, and she was never alive the way that people are here."

"Skeleton people generally aren't," said Jack, setting her cocoa aside. "If they were, I would expect them to die instantly, due to their lack of functional respiration or circulatory systems. The lack of tendons alone—"

"You must be a lot of fun at parties," said Christopher.

Jack smirked. "It depends on the kind of party. If there

are shovels involved, I'm the life, death, and resurrection of the place."

"I can't go home," said Nancy. She looked down at her cocoa. "My parents . . . they're like Christopher's, I guess. They love me. But they didn't understand me *before* I went away, and now, I might as well be from another planet. They keep trying to get me to wear colors and eat every day, and go on dates with boys like nothing ever happened. Like everything is just the way it used to be. But I didn't want to go on dates with boys before I went to the Underworld, and I don't want to do it now. I won't. I *can't.*"

Kade looked a little hurt. "No one is going to make you do anything you don't want to do," he said, and his tone was stiff and wounded.

Nancy shook her head. "That's not what I mean. I don't want to go on dates with girls, either. I don't want to go on dates with *anyone*. People are pretty, sure, and I like to look at pretty things, but I don't want to go on a date with a painting."

"Oh," said Kade, understanding replacing stiffness. He smiled a little. Nancy, glancing up from her cocoa, smiled back. "Well, looks like we've all got good reason to keep this school open. We've had two deaths. Sumi and Loriel. What did they have in common?"

"Nothing," said Christopher. "Sumi went to a Mirror, Loriel went to a Fairyland. High Nonsense and high Logic. They didn't hang out together, they didn't have friends in common, they didn't do any of the same things for fun. Sumi liked origami and making friendship bracelets, Loriel did puzzles and paint-by-numbers. They only overlapped in class and during meals, and I'm pretty sure they would have stopped doing that if they'd been able to. They weren't enemies. They were just . . . disinterested."

"Nancy said something before about Sumi's hands being the most important things about her," said Kade.

Jack sat up straighter. "Why, Nancy, how callous and odd of you."

Nancy reddened. "I'm sorry. I just . . . I just thought . . ."

"Oh, that wasn't a complaint. It's just that usually, if someone around here is going to be callous and odd, it's me." Jack frowned thoughtfully. "You may be onto something there. Each of us has some attribute that attracted the attention of our door in the first place, some inherent point of sympathy that made it possible for us to be happy on the other side. It's an assumption, I know, built on seeing only the survivors—maybe most of those who go through the doors never return, and so what we see is only ever the best-case scenario. Either way, we'd need to have *something* to get us through the story alive. And for many people, that intangible *something* seems to have been concentrated in a certain part of the body."

"Like Loriel's eyes," said Kade.

Jack nodded. "Yes, or Nancy's incredibly robust musculature—don't look at me like that, you need very strong muscles to stand without collapsing for the sort of times you've described—or Angela's legs, or Seraphina's beauty. The girl's a rancid bucket of leeches on the inside, but she has a face that could move angels to murder. I've seen pictures from before she went traveling. She was always pretty. She was no Helen of Troy, until she traveled."

"How have you seen pictures from before she went traveling?" asked Kade.

"I have the Internet, and her Facebook password is the name of her cat, which she has a picture of above her bed." Jack snorted. "I am a genius of infinite potential and highly limited patience. People shouldn't try me so."

"I'll keep that in mind the next time I'm trying to keep a secret," said Kade. "What are you saying?"

"I'm saying that back when I worked for Dr. Bleak, sometimes he wanted me to gather things for him," said Jack. "Only the best would do, which was absolutely right and fair: he was a genius, too, a greater genius than I can ever dream of being. So he'd say 'I need six bats,' and I would spend days with a net out on the moor, catching the very best, biggest bats, and bring him the finest specimens for his work. Or he might say 'I need a golden carp without a single silver scale,' and I'd spend a week by the river, netting fish after fish, until I had something perfect. Those were the easy jobs. Other times he'd say 'I need a perfect dog, but you're never going to *find* a perfect dog, so go out and find the parts I need.' Head and haunches, tail and toes, I'd have to gather them wherever they were found, and bring them back to him."

"Okay, first, that's gross," said Christopher. "Second, that's inhumane. Third, what are you saying? That some mad scientist is trying to build a perfect girl out of the best parts of us?"

"I'm the only mad scientist at this school, and I'm not killing people," said Jack. "Apart from that? Yes. I'm saying that sometimes, murder isn't about the bodies, or the dead. Those are the things that are left behind. Sometimes, murder is about what's *missing*."

There was a knock at the attic door. Everyone jumped, even Jack. Cocoa slopped over the side of Nancy's cup. Jack sat up straight, putting her cup down and tensing, like a snake getting ready to strike. Kade cleared his throat.

"Who is it?" he called.

"Jill." The doorknob turned. The door swung open. Jill stepped inside. She looked curiously around before announcing, "I looked for you, and when I didn't find you, I decided to come here, since it was the highest point in the house and the closest to the sun, which made it the least likely place for you to be. Now there you are, and here I am. Why did you run off and leave me alone for so long?"

"I was disposing of the body, as I had been asked." Jack slid off her perch, straightening her vest with a quick tug, and said, "Speaking of the body, the acid should be finished with Loriel's soft tissues by this point. Christopher, did you want to come help me with her bones?"

"Sure," said Christopher, sounding bemused. He stood, setting his cocoa aside, and followed Jack out of the attic.

Jill didn't say anything as her sister walked away and left her. She just turned a bright, guileless smile on Kade, and asked, "Is there any more of that cocoa?"

8 HER SKELETON, IN RAINBOWS CLAD

JACK DESCENDED THE STAIRS as if they had personally challenged her, taking them two and three at a time, until Christopher had to jog to keep pace. Throughout her flight, she never seemed to be working: she remained perfectly serene, cold-eyed and thin-lipped, not breathing hard or struggling in the slightest. She didn't speak. Christopher was worried, but also grateful. He wasn't sure he would have been able to answer her without gasping.

"Do we need to clean the bones before you call them?" she asked, as they walked the last length of hallway between the last stretch of stairs and the basement. There were no students there. They hadn't seen any students since leaving the attic. The campus would have seemed deserted, if not for the whispers still drifting from behind closed doors. "Acid is pretty, but it's not a good thing to dress a dancer."

"No," said Christopher, taking the bone flute from his pocket and wrapping his fingers around it, as much for reassurance as for anything else. "She'll rise up clean and lovely. Back in the Country of the Bones, we would free new citizens by—" He stopped midsentence, like he'd just realized he was about to say something horrible.

Jack looked back at him as she opened the basement door. "All right, now I'm genuinely curious. You have to tell me. Don't worry about upsetting me, I once removed a man's lungs from his chest while he was still alive, awake, and trying to talk."

"Why would you do something like that?"

"Why wouldn't I?" Jack shrugged and started down the stairs.

Christopher stared after her for a moment before he started moving again. When he caught up, he said defiantly, "We freed new citizens by cutting through their flesh. Big, deep cuts, all the way down to the bone. That way the skeletons within could rise up without having to struggle and risk fracturing themselves. Bones heal slow, even outside the body."

"The fact that the bones healed at all is the strange thing to me," said Jack. Her voice was quiet. "The rules were so *different* there. For all of us."

"Yeah," agreed Christopher, looking at the reddish liquid filling the tub. A few chunks floated on the surface. He didn't want to think about them too hard.

"You shouldn't tell anyone what you just told me. The petty-minded fools here think surgery and butchery are the same thing. Look at the way they look at me. Right now, you're still one of them, but don't make the mistake of thinking that can't change." Jack walked across the room to the wardrobe. "Everything changes."

"I know," said Christopher, and raised his flute to his lips, and began to play.

There was no sound, not that the living could hear: there was only the *idea* of sound, the sudden, overwhelming sensation that something was being overlooked, something small and subtle and hidden between the molecules of silence. Jack opened the wardrobe and took out a cravat, listening as hard as she could as she removed her bow tie. She heard her own breathing. She heard Christopher's fingers brushing across bone. She heard a splash.

She turned around.

Christopher was still playing, and Loriel was sitting up, a polished bone sculpture. Her scapulae were delicate wings; her skull was a psalm to the elegant dancer waiting beneath the flesh of all who walked the earth. There was a pearlescent sheen to her, like opal, and Jack wondered idly whether that was the acid or the magic of Christopher's flute at work. It was a pity she would probably never know. The school, pleasant as it was, didn't exactly go out of its way to provide her with bodies to examine.

Slowly, gingerly, Loriel's bones stood, wobbling slightly, and climbed out of the tub. A single drop of acid rolled from her elbow and fell to the floor, where it hissed as it ate a pit in the stone. She stopped, rocking from side to side, her empty eye sockets fixed on Christopher.

"That's amazing," said Jack, taking a step forward. "Can she see you? Is she *aware*? Or is this just magic animating her bones? Does it work on any skeleton, or just those who died violently? Can you—you can't answer any of my questions unless you stop playing, can you?"

Christopher shook his head and gestured with an elbow toward the stairs that would lead to the old servant's door. Jack nodded.

"I'll get them open," she said, and trotted off, tying the cravat as she went. Her fingers, while not as nimble as Sumi's, were quick, and the knot was a familiar one; by the time she reached the door and shoved it open, she was once more impeccably dressed. Of all the skills she'd learned from Dr. Bleak, the ability to groom herself while running for her life seemed the most likely to continue to serve her well in this strange, often confusing world she presently called "home."

Christopher followed her more sedately, playing his silent flute all the way. Loriel trailed after him, her toes tapping on the stairs, making a sound that was virtually indistinguishable from the clatter of dried branches on a windowpane. Jack stood and watched as the pair walked outside, and then she followed, closing the door.

"Are we looking for a place to bury her where she won't be found?" she asked. Christopher nodded. "Follow me, then."

Together, they walked across the property, the girl, the boy, and the dancing skeleton wrapped in rainbows. Neither of those who still possessed tissue and tongue spoke.

This was the closest thing Loriel would have to a funeral; it would have been inappropriate to make light of it. They walked until they came to the place where the landscaping dropped away, replaced by tangle and weed, and the hard stretch of stony earth that had never been farmed or claimed as anything other than wilderness. Eleanor West owned it all, of course: her family had owned the countryside for miles around, and now that she was the last, every inch of it belonged to her. She had simply refused to sell or allow development on any of the lots surrounding her school. The local conservationists considered her a hero. The local capitalists considered her an enemy. Some of her greatest detractors said she acted like a woman with something to hide, and they were right, in their way; she was a woman with something to protect. That made her more dangerous than they could ever have suspected.

"Wait," said Jack, when they reached the waste. She turned to Loriel, and said, "If you can hear me, if you can understand me, nod. Please. I know you didn't like me when you were alive, and I didn't like you either, but there are lives on the line. Save them. Answer me."

Christopher kept playing. Slowly, Loriel's skull dipped toward her sternum, moving in the absence of muscles or tendons to command it. Jack blew out a breath.

"See, this could be a Ouija situation, where any answers I get from you are just the things Christopher wants me to hear, but I don't think that's the case," she said. "Maybe it would have been a week ago, but Nancy's at the school now, and ghosts want to be near her. I think you're still Loriel, on some level, deep down. So please, if you can, tell me. Who killed you?"

Loriel was still for several seconds. Then, slowly, as if every move were an impossible effort, she raised her right arm and pointed her index finger at the space next to Jack. Jack turned to look at the empty air. Then she sighed.

"I suppose that was too much to ask," she said. "Christopher?"

He nodded, and moved his fingers on the flute. Loriel's skeleton walked down the short hill into the waste—and kept walking downward, her steps carrying her into and through the ground, as if she were walking on an unseen stairway. In less than a minute, she was gone, the crown of her head vanishing below the soil. Christopher lowered his flute.

"She was so beautiful," he said.

"I'd find that less creepy if I thought you were talking about her with the skin on," said Jack. "Come on. Let's get back to the others. It's not safe to be alone." She turned, and Christopher followed her, and they trudged together across the wide green lawn.

9 THE BROKEN BIRDS OF AVALON

LUNCH WAS A STILTED affair, with no one talking and few students actually eating. For once, Nancy's preference for sipping fruit juice and pushing the solid food around her plate without tasting it didn't come across as strange; if anything, the strange part was her willingness to ingest anything at all. She found herself scanning the other students, trying to guess at their stories, their hidden worlds, to figure out what, if anything, would drive them to kill. Maybe if she had been there longer, if they hadn't been such strangers to her, she would have been able to find the answers she needed. As it was, it felt like she wasn't able to find anything but questions.

After lunch there was an assembly in the library, where Miss Eleanor praised everyone for their calm and their compassion, and thanked Jack, Nancy, and the others for disposing of Loriel's body. Nancy reddened and sank lower in her seat, trying to avoid the eyes that were turning toward her. *She* was a stranger, as far as they were concerned, and as such, her willingness to be intimate with the dead had to be suspicious.

Eleanor took a deep breath and looked out upon the room—her students, her charges—with a somber expression on her face. "As you all know, my door is still open," she said. "My world is a Nonsense world, with high Virtue and moderate Rhyme as its crosswise directions. Many of you wouldn't be able to survive there. The lack of logic and reason would destroy you. But for those of you who thrive in Nonsense, I am willing to open the door and let you go through. You can hide there, for a time."

A gasp ran through the room, accompanied by a few quick, choked-off sobs. A girl with bright blue hair bent double, burying her face against her knees and starting to rock back and forth, like she could soothe her distress away. One of the boys got up and went to the corner, turning his back on everyone. Worse were the ones who simply sat and wept, tears running down their faces, hands folded tightly in their laps.

Nancy looked blankly at Kade. He sighed and leaned closer to her.

"Miss Eleanor is very protective of her door. Doors can be fickle, and she's waited so long to go back that every time she lets someone through, she risks being replaced. Now she's offering to put all the students who can thrive in Nonsense through. That means she's scared, and she's doing what she can to take care of us." He kept his voice low. The students around them didn't seem to notice. Most were too busy crying. On the other side of the room, even Jill was weeping, propped against her sister for support. Only Jack's eyes were dry. "Trouble is, Nonsense is one of the two big directions—she can save half the students, at best, and not everyone who's been to a Nonsense world is suited for *every* Nonsense world. They're all so different. Maybe a quarter of the kids she's just offered to save will be able to go through."

"Oh," said Nancy softly. She understood a few things about false hope, however well-intentioned the offer might have been. Eleanor was trying to save her beloved charges in the only way she knew. She was hurting them in the process.

At the head of the room, Eleanor took a shaky breath. "As always, my darlings, attendance at this school is purely voluntary. If any of you want to call your parents and ask them to take you home, I will refund the rest of the fees for the semester, and I won't try to stop you. I only ask that, for the sake of the students who remain, you don't tell them why you want to withdraw. We'll find a way to fix this."

"Oh, yeah?" asked Angela bitterly. "Can you fix it for Loriel?"

Eleanor looked away. "Get to class," she said. Her voice was soft, and suddenly old.

She stood there, head bowed, as the students rose and filed out. Some were still crying. She would seek out the Nonsense children soon, tap them on their shoulders and lead them to her door. Some would be able to go through, she was sure. There were always a few for whom her world was close enough. Still not home, not the checkerboard sky or mirrored sea that they were dreaming of, but . . . close enough. Close enough for them to be happy, for them to start to live again. And who knew? Doors opened every-where. Maybe one day, the children of this world who had gone to that world to save themselves would see a door that didn't fit right with the walls around it, something with a doorknob made of a moon, or a knocker that winked. Maybe they could still go home.

A hand touched her shoulder. She turned to find Kade behind her, a worried expression on his face. She glanced toward the seats, and there was Nancy, retreated once more into stillness. It didn't matter. There were too many secrets here to be shy about revealing them. Eleanor turned to Kade once more and buried her face against his chest, weeping.

"It's all right, Aunt Ely, it's all right," said Kade, strok-ing her back with one hand. "We're going to figure this out."

"My students are *dying*, Kade," she said. "They're dying, and I can get so few of them out of harm's way. I can't save you. When you found your door, I thought—"

"I know," he said. "It's too bad for all of us that I have a Logical heart." He kept stroking her back. "It'll be okay. You'll see. We'll figure this out, we'll find a way, and we'll keep the doors open, no matter what."

Eleanor sighed, pulling away. "You're a good boy, Kade. Your parents don't know what they're missing."

His smile in response was sad. "That's the trouble, Auntie. They know exactly what they're missing, and since she's never going to be found again, they don't know what to do with me."

"Silly child," said Eleanor. "Now get to class."

"Getting," he said, and walked toward the door. Nancy shook off her statue stillness and followed him.

She waited until they were halfway down the hall before she said, "Eleanor is your . . . ?"

"Great-great-great-aunt," said Kade. "She never married or had children. Her sister, on the other hand, had six. Since my great-great-great-grandma had a husband to take care of her, Eleanor inherited the entire estate. I'm the first of her nieces or nephews to find a door of my own. She was so happy thinking that I'd traveled into Nonsense that it took me almost a month to admit she was typing me wrong, and I'd been in a world of pure Logic. She loves me anyway. Someday, all this"—he gestured to the walls around them—"will be mine, and the school will stay open for another few decades. Assuming we don't close in the next week."

"I'm sure we won't," said Nancy. "We'll figure this out."

"Before the authorities get involved?"

Nancy didn't have an answer to that.

CLASSES WERE PERFUNCTORY and distracted, taught by instructors who could sense that the campus was uneasy, even if they didn't—except for Lundy—know why. Dinner was

equally rushed, the beef overcooked and dry, the fruit sliced
so haphazardly that bits of peel and rind stuck to the outside when it was served. Students went off in threes and
fours, arranging impromptu sleepovers with their friends.
Nancy didn't bat an eye when Kade and Christopher
showed up at her room clutching sleeping bags and flipped
a coin for the use of Sumi's bed. Kade won and settled on
the mattress, while Christopher rolled his bedding out
on the floor. All three of them closed their eyes and pre-
tended to sleep—a pretense that, for Nancy, became reality
sometime after midnight.

She dreamt of ghosts, and silent halls where the dead
walked, untroubled.

Christopher dreamt of dancing skeletons that gleamed
like opals, and the unchanging, ever-welcoming smile of
the Skeleton Girl.

Kade dreamt a world in all the colors of the rainbow, a
prism of a country, shattering itself into a thousand shards
of light. He dreamt himself home and welcomed as he
was, not as they had wanted him to be, and of the three, he
was the one who cried into his pillow and woke, cheeks wet,
to the sound of screaming.

It was a far-off sound, coming from somewhere outside
the window; Nancy and Christopher were still asleep,
which only made sense. They had come from worlds where
screams were more common, and less dangerous, than they
were here. Kade sat up, wiping the sleep from his eyes, and
waited for the screams to come again. They did not. He
hesitated.

Should he wake them, take them with him when he went to investigate? Nancy was already under suspicion by most of her peers, and Christopher would be too, if he kept getting involved. Kade could go alone. Most of the students liked him, since he was the one who kept the wardrobe in order, and they would forgive him for finding another body. But then he'd be alone, and if either Nancy or Christopher woke before he got back, they would worry. He didn't want to worry them.

Kade knelt and shook Christopher by the shoulder. The other boy groaned before opening his eyes and squinting up at Kade. "What is it?" he asked, voice heavy with sleep.

"Somebody just screamed out near the trees," said Kade. "We need to go see why."

Christopher sat up, seeming instantly awake. "Are we taking Nancy?"

"Yes," said Nancy, sliding out of her bed. Screams hadn't been enough to wake her, but speech had: in the Halls of the Dead, no one spoke unless they wanted to be listened to. "I don't want to stay here alone."

Neither of the boys argued. All of them shared the same fear of being left alone in this suddenly haunted house, where the ghosts were nothing they could understand.

They walked quietly, but they didn't creep, all of them secretly hoping someone would wake, come out of their room, and join the small processional. Instead, the doors stayed shut, and the trio found themselves walking alone toward the shadowy grove where Nancy and Jill had sought shelter from the unforgiving sun. There was no sunlight now: only the moon, looking down from between the patches in the clouds.

Then they stepped into the trees, and the moonlight became too much to bear, for the moonlight was enough to show Lundy, lying small and silent on the ground, her eyes open and staring into the leaves. *She* still had her eyes and her hands, and seemed to have everything else. Her clothes were unbloodied, her limbs intact.

"Lundy," said Kade, and moved to kneel beside her, reaching for a pulse. The motion caused her head to roll to the side, revealing what had been taken.

Kade scrabbled away, shambling to his feet, before running to the other side of the clearing and vomiting noisily into the bushes. Nancy and Christopher, who were less disturbed by gore, looked at the empty bowl of Lundy's skull and stepped a little closer together, shivering despite the warmth of the night.

"Why would someone take her *brain?*" asked Nancy.

"I was about to ask you the same question," snarled Angela.

Nancy and Christopher turned. Angela was standing at the edge of the grove, a flashlight in her hand and several shadow-draped students behind her. Shining the light directly in Nancy's eyes, she demanded, "Where is Seraphina?"

"Who's Seraphina?" asked Nancy, raising a hand to shade her eyes. She heard footsteps a moment before Kade's hand settled on her shoulder. She took a half step back, letting him shelter her. "We came out here because we heard screaming."

"You came out here to hide the body," snapped Angela. "Where is she?"

"Seraphina is the prettiest girl in school, Nancy—you've seen her. She traveled to a Nonsense world, high Wicked, high Rhyme," said Kade. "Pretty as a sunrise, mean as a snake. She ain't here, Angela." His Oklahoma accent was suddenly strong, dominating his words. "Go back to your room. I have to go wake Miss Eleanor. Odds are good she's let Seraphina through her door."

"If she hasn't, you better give her back," said Angela. "If you hurt her, I will kill you."

"We don't have her," said Christopher. "We were asleep up until five minutes ago."

"Who's that with you?" asked Kade. "Have you just been roaming the campus looking for someone to accuse? You're out here as much as we are. This could be your handiwork."

"We went to good, respectable worlds," said Angela. "Moonbeams and rainbows and unicorn tears, not . . . not skeletons and dead people and deciding to be boys when we're really girls!"

Sudden silence fell over the grove. Even Angela's supporters seemed stunned by her words. Angela paled.

"I didn't mean that," she said.

"Oh, but I believe you did," said Eleanor. She stepped around Angela and the others, walking slowly to where Lundy was sprawled in the dirt. She was leaning on a cane.

That was new, as were some of the lines in her cheeks. She seemed to be aging by the day. "Ah, my poor Lundy. I suppose this may have been a kinder death than the one you were looking forward to, but I still wish you hadn't gone."

"Ma'am—" began Kade.

"All of you, go back to your rooms," said Eleanor. "Angela, we'll speak in the morning. For now, stay together and try to survive the night." She braced both hands on her cane and stayed where she was, looking down at Lundy's body. "My poor girl."

"But—"

"I am still headmistress here, at least until I'm dead," said Eleanor. "Go."

They went.

Their tiny group managed to stay together until they had reached the front steps. Then Angela turned on Kade, and said, "I meant what I said. It's sick, how you pretend like you're something you're not."

"I was about to say the same thing to you," said Christopher. "I mean, you always did a pretty good job of pretending to be a decent human being. You had me fooled."

Angela gaped at him. Then she turned and stormed up the stairs, with her friends at her heels. Nancy turned to Kade, who shook his head.

"It's all right," he said. "Let's go back to bed."

"I would prefer if you didn't," said Jack.

The three of them turned. The usually dapper mad scientist was standing by the corner of the house, drenched in blood, clutching her left shoulder with her right hand. Blood trickled from between her fingers, bright enough to be visible in the gloom. Her tie was undone. Somehow, that was the worst part of all.

"I seem to need assistance," she said, and pitched forward in a dead faint.

10 BE STILL AS STONE, AND YOU MAY LIVE

KADE AND CHRISTOPHER gathered Jack up; Kade and Christopher carried Jack away, while Nancy stood, frozen and temporarily forgotten, in the shadows on the porch. She knew, in an academic way, that she should hurry after them—that she shouldn't stand out here alone, where anything could happen to her. But that seemed hasty, and dangerous. Stillness was safer. Stillness had saved her before, and it would save her now.

She had forgotten how much like pomegranate juice a bloodstain could look, in the right light.

She had forgotten how beautiful it was.

So now: stand still, so still that she became one with the background, that she could feel her heart slowing, five beats becoming four, becoming three, until there was no more than one beat per minute, until she barely had to breathe.

Maybe Jack was right; maybe her ability to be still was pre-ternaturally honed. It didn't feel like anything special. It just felt *correct,* as if this was what she should have been all the time, always.

Her parents worried because she didn't eat enough, and maybe that was something they needed to worry about when she was moving like a hot, fast thing, but they didn't understand. She wasn't going to stay here, in their hot, fast world. She *wasn't.* And when she slowed her body down like this, when she was *still,* she didn't need to eat any more than she already did. She could survive for a century on a spoonful of juice, a crumb of cake, and consider herself well-nourished. She didn't have an eating disorder. She knew what she needed, and what she needed was to be still.

Nancy breathed deeper into her stillness and felt her heart stop for the span of a minute, becoming as motion-less as the rest of her, like a pomegranate seed nestled safe at the center of a fruit. She was preparing to take another breath, to let her heart enjoy another beat, when someone stepped around the corner of the house. Nancy would have said that she couldn't become any more motionless. In that moment, she proved herself wrong. In that moment, she was as still and as inconsequential as stone.

Jill walked past the porch, bloodstains on her hands and a parasol slung over one shoulder, blocking out any errant rays of moonlight that might dare caress her skin. There was a drop of blood at the corner of her mouth, like a spot of jam that her napkin had missed. As Nancy watched, motionless, Jill's little pink tongue flicked out and wiped the blood away. Jill kept walking. Nancy didn't move.

Please, she thought. *Please, my Lord, keep my heart from beating. Please, don't let her see me.*

Nancy's heart did not beat.

Jill walked around the far corner of the house and was gone.

Nancy breathed in. Her lungs ached at the invasion of air; her heart protested as it started to pound, going from stillness to a race in under a second. It took a few seconds more for the blood to resume circulating through her body, and then she spun and ran for the house, following the drops of blood on the floor until she reached the heretofore unseen kitchen and burst through the door.

Kade whirled, a carving knife in his hand. Christopher stepped in front of Eleanor. Jack was lying motionless on the butcher's block in the middle of the room, her shirt cut away and makeshift bandages covering the stab wound in her arm.

"Nancy?" Kade lowered the knife. "What happened?"

"I *saw* her," gasped Nancy. "I saw Jill. She did this."

"Yes," said Jack wearily. "She did."

11 YOU CAN NEVER GO HOME

JACK'S EYES WERE OPEN and fixed on the ceiling. Slowly, she used her uninjured arm to push herself upright. When Christopher stepped forward as if to help, she waved him off, muttering an irritated, "I am injured, not an invalid. Some things I must do myself." He backed away. She finished sitting and held that position for a moment, head bowed, fighting to get her breath back.

No one moved. Finally, Jack said, "I should have seen it sooner. I suppose I did, on some level, but I didn't *want* to, so I refused it as best I could. She makes it out like it was my fault we had to leave the Moors, like the work I was doing with Dr. Bleak riled up the villagers. That's not true. Dr. Bleak and I never killed anyone—not on purpose—and most of the locals left us their bodies when they died, because they knew we could use the bits they'd

left behind to save lives. We were *doctors*. She's the one who
went and became beloved of a monster. She's the one
who wanted to be just. Like. Him."

"Jack . . . ?" said Kade, warily.

Nancy, who remembered the moonlight glittering off a
speck of blood like jam, said nothing.

"She would have made a beautiful monster, if she'd been
a little smarter," said Jack quietly. "She certainly had the
appetite for it. Eventually, I suppose she would have learnt
subtlety. But she didn't learn fast enough, and they found
out what she was doing, and they took up their torches and
they marched, and Dr. Bleak knew she'd never be forgiven.
He drugged her. He opened the door and went to throw
her through. I couldn't let her go alone. She's my *sister*. I
just didn't know how *hard* it would be."

"Sweetheart, what are you saying?" asked Eleanor.

Nancy, who remembered the way Jill had smiled when
she talked about her Master, and how far she'd been willing to go to please him, said nothing.

"It's my sister." Jack looked at Kade rather than Eleanor, like it was easier for her to say this to a peer. "She killed
them all. She's trying to build herself a key. We have to stop
her." She slid off the butcher block, only wincing a little
when the impact of her feet hitting the floor traveled up
through her bad arm. "Seraphina is still alive."

"That's why Loriel pointed next to you, but not at you,"
said Christopher.

Jack nodded. "I didn't kill her. She knew it. Jill did."

"I saw her outside," said Nancy. "She was walking like there was no hurry. Where would she go?"

"She stabbed me in the basement, but she'll be heading for the attic," said Jack. She grimaced. "The skylights . . . it's easier when there's a storm. I tried to stop her. I tried."

"It's all right," said Kade. "We've got it from here."

"You're not going without me," said Jack. "She's my sister."

"Can you keep up?"

Jack's smile was thin and strained. "Try to stop me."

Kade glanced to Eleanor, expression questioning. She closed her eyes.

"Jack can keep up, but I can't," she said. "Don't go if you're not sure that you'll come back to me."

They went.

The four students ran through the house, fleet and angry. Jack was surprisingly steady on her feet, given the amount of blood she had lost. Nancy brought up the rear. Stillness and speed were diametrically opposed. But she did the best she could, and they all reached the attic door at roughly the same time. Kade slammed the door open.

Jill was standing in an ocean of books with a knife in her hand. The table she had swept clear was now occupied by Seraphina—the most beautiful girl in the world—and an assortment of jars, each with its own, terrible burden. Jill raised her head as the door opened, and sighed. "Go *away*," she said peevishly. "This is delicate work. I don't have time for you."

Kade was the first to step into the room, his hands held out in front of him. "You don't want to do this."

"I think I do," Jill countered. "You don't know me. None of you know me. Not even her." She jerked her chin at Jack. "I'm going *home*. I'm going back to my Master. I figured out the way, and no one can stop me. If you try, they'll have all died in vain, and I'll just do it again. I'm going to build my skeleton key."

Seraphina whimpered behind the gag that covered her mouth, eyes rolling wildly as she looked for a way out. She wasn't finding one.

"The door home is locked for a reason," said Jack. "You can't get around that."

"But I can, dear sister, *I can,*" said Jill. "Everyone here has something special about them, something that called the doors. I'm building the perfect girl. The girl who has everything. The smartest, prettiest, fastest, strongest girl. Every door will open for her. Every world will want her. And when I get to the Moors, I'll kill her, and I'll be allowed to stay forever. I just want to go home. Surely you can appreciate that."

"We all do," said Christopher. "This isn't the way."

"There isn't any other," said Jill.

"The dead aren't tools," said Nancy, stepping past Kade with her hands held loosely at her sides. "Please. You're hurting them. You're stealing the things that make them important because you want a skeleton key, but they can't move on to their afterlives until you give those things back." She didn't know that her words were true, but they felt so *right* that she didn't question them. "Why is your happy-ever-after the only one that matters?"

"Because I'm the one who's willing to take it," snapped Jill. "Back off, or she dies, and I tell everyone it was you. Who are they going to believe? The ingénue, or the girl who talks to ghosts? Even your supporters are weird. I'll come out smelling like a rose, just you watch."

Jill's eyes were fixed on Nancy. She didn't see Jack move away from the others, making her slow way around the edge of the attic. Christopher and Kade were silent.

"You know this is wrong, Jill," said Nancy. "You know the dead are angry with you."

Jack continued to move, slow and easy and quiet as a prayer. She picked up a pair of scissors.

"I don't care about the dead," said Jill. "I care about going *home*. I care about my Master. I care about my*self*, and the rest of you can hang, as far as I'm—" She stopped in the middle of her sentence, making a small choking sound. She looked down as blood began to spread through the front of her lacy peignoir. Then, gracelessly, she collapsed, revealing the scissors sticking out of her back.

Jack looked down at her fallen sister for a moment. Her eyes were dry when she raised her head and looked at the others. "I'm sorry," she said. "I should have understood faster. I should have seen it. I didn't. I apologize."

"You killed your sister." Nancy sounded puzzled. "Did you have to . . . ?"

"Murder trials are so messy, aren't they? And death isn't forever if you know what you're doing. Jill was the one

Dr. Bleak locked the door against, not me. I've always been welcome at home, if I was willing to leave her behind . . . or change her. Her Master won't want her now. Once you've died and been resurrected, you can't be a vampire." Jack bent to pull the scissors from Jill's back. They came up dripping red. She grimaced as the blood oozed onto her fingers. "If you'll forgive me, we must be going. So much to do, and resurrections always work better when they're performed quickly. I can bring her back. She'll still be my sister."

She slashed the bloody scissors through the air. They cut lines in the nothingness, until a rectangle hung open next to her, showing a dark, wind-racked field. In the distance, a castle, with a village at its base. Jack's face softened, becoming suffused with unspeakable longing.

"Home," she breathed. She bent, sliding her arms under Jill—grunting slightly as the motion reopened the slash in her left shoulder—and lifting her sister's body in a bridal carry. She stepped through the door. She didn't look back.

The last any of them saw of the sisters was Jack, suddenly distant and so small on that vast, empty plain, walking through the darkness toward the castle lights. Then the rectangle faded, leaving them alone in the attic once again.

Seraphina whimpered behind her gag. Time resumed. Time had a way of doing that.

AND THEY ALL LIVED

WITHOUT JACK TO HELP, disposing of Lundy's body was more difficult: no one really wanted to go into the basement save for Christopher and Nancy, and they didn't know enough about chemicals to dissolve her safely. In the end, she was laid to rest in the grove where she'd been killed, buried deep among the tree roots. Sumi's hands and Loriel's eyes were buried with her. The police pursued a few false leads looking for Sumi's killer, but eventually they admitted that the trail had gone cold, and the case was closed.

Eleanor was slow to recover her vitality; she still walked with a cane, although she was sturdy enough to run the school without her right-hand woman and best friend. Kade began stepping up to fill the void Lundy had left. More and more, it was obvious that one day, the school would be his—and that he would do a good job. Eleanor's legacy would be protected, as it always should have been.

Nancy moved into the basement, once it had been thoroughly cleaned out. Seraphina had repeated the story of her rescue often enough that the other students no longer blamed Nancy or her friends for the deaths; while they might not be friends, at least they weren't enemies.

The rest of the semester passed like a dream. Nancy was packing to go home when she heard footsteps on the stairs and turned to see Kade standing there, a familiar flowered suitcase in his hand.

"Hey," he said.

"Hey," she replied.

"Heard you were going home for the holidays."

Nancy nodded. "My parents insisted." They had begged, they had pleaded with her over the phone, and every word had solidified her determination not to do anything that would give them an excuse to pull her out of school. She didn't want to stay here, where it was bright and colorful and fast, but she would take a thousand school days over a single day in the presence of her parents, who would never understand.

She couldn't even be excited at the thought of seeing them again. During her days among the dead, she had wondered what her family was doing, whether they missed her; now she just wondered if they'd ever let her go.

"I thought you might want to take this"—he held out the suitcase—"so they wouldn't think we'd been encouraging your weirdness."

"That's very kind of you." Nancy smiled as she walked over to take the case from him. "Will you be all right without me?"

"Oh, always," he said. "Christopher and I are working on a new map for worlds connected to the dead. I'm starting to think that maybe Vitus and Mortis are minor directions. That might explain a few things."

"I'll look forward to seeing your work," said Nancy gravely.

"Cool." Kade took a step back up the stairs. "Have a good vacation, okay?"

"I will," said Nancy. She watched him walk away. When the door shut behind him, she closed her eyes and allowed herself a few seconds of stillness, centering her thoughts.

So this was the world. This was the place she'd come from—and more, this was the place where she came closest to belonging *in* this world. She could stay at the school until she graduated, and after. She could be Kade's Lundy, once Eleanor was gone, to Nonsense or to the grave; she could be the woman who stood beside him and helped to keep things going. She'd do a better job, she thought, of telling the students about their futures without making those futures seem like life sentences. She could learn to be happy here, if she had to. But never completely. That would be too much to ask.

She opened her eyes and looked at the suitcase in her hands before she walked over and set it on Jack's old autopsy table, now blunted with a plain white sheet. The latches resisted a little as she pressed them open and revealed the welter of brightly colored clothes that her parents had packed for her all those months ago.

There was an envelope on top of the tangled blouses and skirts and undergarments. Carefully, Nancy picked it up and opened it, pulling out the note inside.

You're nobody's rainbow.

You're nobody's princess.

You're nobody's doorway but your own, and the only one who gets to tell you how your story ends is you.

Sumi's name wasn't signed: it was scrawled, in big, jagged letters that took up half the page. Nancy laughed, the sound turning into something like a sob. Sumi must have written it that first day, just in case Nancy couldn't handle it; in case she became less sure, and started trying to forget.

Nobody gets to tell me how my story ends but me, she thought, and the words were true enough that she repeated them aloud: "Nobody gets to tell me how my story ends but me."

The air in the room seemed to shift.

The letter still in her hand, Nancy turned. The stairs were gone. There was a doorway in their place, solid oak and so familiar. Slowly, as in a dream, she walked toward it, Sumi's letter falling from her hand and drifting to the floor.

At first, the knob refused to turn. She closed her eyes again, hoping as hard as she could, and felt it give beneath her hand. This time, when she opened her eyes and twisted, the door swung open, and she found herself looking at a grove of pomegranate trees.

The air smelled so sweet, and the sky was black velvet, spangled with diamond stars. Nancy was shaking as she stepped through. The grass was wet with dew, tickling her ankles. She bent to untie her shoes, stepping out of them and leaving them where they lay. The dew coated her toes as she reached up to pluck a pomegranate from the nearest branch. It was so ripe that it had split down the middle, revealing a row of ruby seeds.

The juice was bitter on her lips. It tasted like heaven.

Nancy began walking down the path between the trees, never looking back. The door was gone long before she broke into a run. It wasn't needed anymore. Like a key that finds its keyhole, Nancy was finally home.

ABOUT THE AUTHOR

Seanan McGuire was born in Martinez, California, and raised in a wide variety of locations, most of which boasted some sort of dangerous native wildlife. Despite her almost magnetic attraction to anything venomous, she somehow managed to survive long enough to acquire a typewriter, a reasonable grasp of the English language, and the desire to combine the two. The fact that she wasn't killed for using her typewriter at three o'clock in the morning is probably more impressive than her lack of death by spider bite.

Often described as a vortex of the surreal, many of Seanan's anecdotes end with things like "and then we got the antivenin" or "but it's okay, because it turned out the water wasn't that deep." She has yet to be defeated in a game of "Who here was bitten by the strangest thing?" and can be amused for hours by almost anything. "Almost anything" includes swamps, long walks, long walks *in* swamps, things that live in swamps, horror movies, strange noises, musical theater, reality TV, comic books, finding pennies on the street, and venomous reptiles. Seanan may be the only person on the planet who admits to using John Kenneth Muir's *Horror Films of the 1980s* as a checklist.

Seanan is the author of the October Daye urban fantasies, the InCryptid urban fantasies, and several other works both stand-alone and in trilogies or duologies. In case that isn't enough, she also writes under the pseudonym Mira Grant.

In her spare time, Seanan records CDs of her original filk music. She is also a cartoonist and draws an irregularly posted autobiographical Web comic, "With Friends Like These . . . ," as well as generating a truly ridiculous number of art cards. Surprisingly enough, she finds time to take multihour walks, blog regularly, watch a sickening amount of television, maintain her Web site, and go to pretty much any movie with the word "blood," "night," "terror," or "attack" in the title. Most people believe she doesn't sleep.

Seanan lives in a creaky old farmhouse in Northern California, which she shares with her cats, Alice and Thomas, a vast collection of creepy dolls and horror movies, and sufficient books to qualify her as a fire hazard. She has strongly held and oft-expressed beliefs about the origins of the Black Death, the X-Men, and the need for chain saws in daily life.

Years of writing blurbs for convention program books

have fixed Seanan in the habit of writing all her bios in the third person, so as to sound marginally less dorky. Stress is on the "marginally." It probably doesn't help that she has so many hobbies.

Seanan was the winner of the 2010 John W. Campbell Award for Best New Writer, and her novel *Feed* (as Mira Grant) was named as one of *Publishers Weekly's* Best Books of 2010. In 2013 she became the first person ever to appear five times on the same Hugo ballot.

www.seananmcguire.com